THE DUDE MUST DIE

In Omaha, they called him English Eddie, a well-mannered deadbeat with no future. When Little Jake hired the dude as tutor for his beautiful daughter, things began to happen, and violently. The Double J party was ambushed while home-bound from Omaha, but Little Jake had also hired a couple of case-hardened Texans. Larry and Stretch called a challenge and emptied their holsters — it was showdown-time for the men who decreed the dude must die.

MARSHALL GROVER

THE DUDE MUST DIE

A Larry & Stretch Western

Complete and Unabridged

LINFORD
Leicester

First published in Australia in 1983 by
Horwitz Grahame Book Pty Limited
Australia

First Linford Edition
published August 1995
by arrangement with
Horwitz Publications Pty Limited
Australia

British Library CIP Data

Grover, Marshall
    Larry & Stretch: the dude must die.
    —Large print ed.—
    Linford western library
    I. Title II. Series
    823 [F]

    ISBN 0–7089–7754–5

Published by
F. A. Thorpe (Publishing) Ltd.
Anstey, Leicestershire

Set by Words & Graphics Ltd.
Anstey, Leicestershire
Printed and bound in Great Britain by
T. J. Press (Padstow) Ltd., Padstow, Cornwall

This book is printed on acid-free paper

1

Little Jake and the Glory Hole

WITHIN ten minutes of drifting into Hortonville, the Lone Star Hellions were catching their first glimpse of the cantankerous Jacob Jarvis, better known in this part of Nebraska as Little Jake. They were destined to meet the runty owner of the Double J ranch, and to remember that meeting for many long years to come.

Finding room for their horses at the hitch-rail fronting the Palace Saloon, the Texans reined up and dismounted.

"Couple tall beers," Larry Valentine decided. "And then we eat."

"Best idea you've had all day," approved Stretch Emerson.

Olaf Bloomfeld, the blond and burly deputy of Horton County, came ambling past as the strangers looped their reins and climbed to the saloon porch. He looked them over and, like many a lawman before him, pegged them for a couple of out-of-work cowpokes. Their demeanor was nonchalant. They moved slowly and stiff-legged in the manner of travelers who had come quite a distance and were glad to be out of the saddle.

It was late afternoon and the porch was in shadow. Had the Texans turned to match Bloomfeld's stare, he might have recognized them, because their weatherbeaten faces had been photographed a time or two, to adorn the front pages of frontier newspapers as well as special bulletins filed in the offices of county sheriffs and town marshals all across the untamed territory west of the Mississippi, all the way north to the Canadian border, all the way south to the Rio Bravo. The poor light on that porch and the fact that neither stranger glanced over his shoulder prevented Bloomfeld's recognizing a couple of celebrities.

"I hear laughin' in there," Stretch remarked, pausing a few feet from the batwings.

"Laughin' sounds fine to me," shrugged Larry. "Means the customers are friendly. Let's hope they stay that way."

For their own good reasons, these nomads traveled wary, keeping their ears cocked and their eyes peeled, every nerve alert for the familiar danger signals. Trouble-prone was the term one journalist had coined to describe them. Wherever they roamed it seemed trouble awaited them or followed, clinging to them as adhesively as a wet slicker. They had been on the drift since the end of the Civil War, always claiming to be law-abiding and peace-loving, but always dogged by fickle Fate, always locking horns with the lawless and, in the process, running foul of every variety of peace officer. Lawmen resented their derisive attitude toward all duly-appointed authority while acknowledging their deadly

3

efficiency. It had to be admitted the Texas Hell-Raisers got results in their own unique, hell-for-leather, wild-swinging way. In battle against rustlers, gunslingers, bank bandits and stage robbers, they fought hard and fast, giving no quarter, asking none.

Larry stepped to the entrance and scanned the barroom. Dark-haired and square-jawed, handsome in a rugged, battered way, he stood 6 feet 3 inches in his high-heeled boots, a brawny wanderer of sometimes belligerent disposition, hefty about the shoulders and chest, but flat-bellied and slim-hipped; it wasn't likely the trouble-shooters would ever become flabby.

"How's it look in there?" asked Stretch.

"A lot of cattlemen," Larry reported. "What they're laughin' at is a couple old timers Indian-wrestlin'."

"Sounds harmless enough," remarked the taller Texan.

Woodville Eustace Emerson, better known as Stretch, was uncommonly tall, a beanpole towering over his partner by a full 3 inches. He packed twice as much Colt as Larry, his matched .45's housed in holsters slung from a buscadero-type cartridge belt. Sandy hair straggled from under his sweat-stained Stetson, crowning a homely visage bordered by jughandle ears. His eyes were blue and his expression guileless; he was inclined to leave all the figuring to his more nimble-witted sidekick.

"And the barkeep looks friendly," Larry observed. "So what're we waitin' for?"

They nudged the batwings open and sauntered in, slapping trail-dust from their well-worn range clothes, moving clear of where the old men sat, elbows firm on a tabletop, hands joined, faces red, sweat beading on their brows and trickling into their grey whiskers. Larry felt for them. They looked to be well on in years, too old for such a strenuous test of strength. While their audience cheered them on, they struggled mightily, right hands quivering back and forth.

"Give up on it, Little Jake!" panted the pudgier one. "Consarn you, I got the advantage. I'm — heftier — then you ever was!"

"If I win . . . " gasped the smaller man, "you'll keep your word — you'll — deed me a half share of the Glory Hole . . . !"

"*If* you win," grinned the pudgy one, exerting greater pressure. "But you never saw the day you would whup me — at *anything*."

The Texans breasted the bar and caught the barkeep's eye. Larry dropped a dollar and pantomimed for two tall beers. While the barkeep obliged, Stretch jerked a thumb toward the group gathered about the table where the old men struggled for supremacy.

"What's that all about, amigo?"

"Indian wrassle," grinned the barkeep.

"We know what it is," frowned Larry. "But what can they win — outside of sprainin' their guts?"

"Strangers, huh?" prodded the barkeep, setting their drinks before them. "Welcome to Hortonville, gents. I'm Tom Gates."

The Texans offered their names, took a pull at their beer and repeated their question.

"Little Jake's been at it for years," Gates explained. "Got this bee in his bonnet. Him and Dan Firestone are neighbors, see? And the Glory Hole's on Hammerhead range, right by the border of Double J."

"Firestone owns Hammerhead," guessed Stretch, "and Double J is Little Jake's outfit."

"That's how it goes," nodded Gates. "And, for as long as I can recall, Little Jake's had this hankerin' to water his stock in that old pond. Plenty water on Double J land. I wouldn't say Jake *needs* the Glory Hole, but he sure *craves* it. He made Dan an offer a long time back, but Dan wouldn't sell. Ever since, he does his damnedest to make Dan change his mind. Bullies him. Threatens him. Tries to win it off of him. Like now, for instance."

He paused to frown at their empty glasses. Larry dropped another coin on the bar, while Stretch reached for the counter lunch and began piling a platter with corn bread, cold cuts and dill pickles.

"Quite an appetite you got — and quite a thirst," Gates commented, as he drew refills.

A whoop and a cheer, a wailed curse from Little Jake indicated the contest was over. The neighboring ranchers rose and advanced to the bar to refuel, the short one still cursing, insisting he was far from licked. Studying him covertly, Larry noted his wispy physique. Small wonder they called him Little Jake. He was no more than 5 feet 2 inches, a grey whiskered, grizzled veteran, shaggy-browed and bulbous-nosed, his frail frame rigged in dusty ranch clothes. He might have passed unnoticed in this crowded barroom but for his personality. Vital was too mild a word to describe him. He radiated energy, impatience and bad temper.

"Real ornery," Stretch quietly remarked, as they toted their food and beer to an unoccupied table. "But kinda likable."

"Proddiest little galoot I've seen in many a long year," declared Larry.

The other rancher, Dan Firestone, looked to be only a couple of inches taller than his neighbor, pudgy but durable, his sugarloaf hat shoved to the back of his head to reveal he was balding fast. His moon face was placid; Larry figured him for a less fiery personality than Little Jake, but just as stubborn. Gates poured two shots of rye. The ranchers swigged them down, and then Little Jake started in again.

"I ain't through yet. Just thought of another way we could settle this thing."

"Consarn your flea-bit hide, ain't you never gonna quit?" Firestone grimaced in exasperation. "You keep tryin' — and you keep losin'. You know you can't outfight me, nor beat me at poker. You know you can't ride any faster'n me. Anything you can do, it seems I can do it just a mite better."

"This time, I'm bettin' my gun-speed against yours," announced Little Jake. To the great amusement of the onlookers, he unholstered his Colt and unloaded it, ejecting the bullets onto the bartop. Firestone shrugged resignedly, drew his pistol and followed his example. "This time *I'll* have the edge, Dan Firestone, on accounta I'm spare built, and you're gonna be slowed down by all that blubber."

"I ain't all that fat," retorted Firestone. "Listen, if I was twice as fat, I could beat your draw — *any* time."

"Best outa three draws — okay?" challenged Little Jake.

"If you can beat my speed just one time," grinned Firestone, "I'll call you half-owner of the Glory Hole, and you can water Double J stock there as often as you please."

"You all heard!" Little Jake bellowed at the assembled cowpokes, and Larry was taken aback; it seemed incredible a voice so thunderous could issue from a man so small. "You're all witnesses! If I outdraw Firestone . . . !"

"Sure, Jake, we all heard." A scrawny redhead nodded impatiently and called advice to the barkeep. "Hey, Tom, you better count them shells. Jake might be keepin' one in his iron — for Dan."

Raising his voice above the uproar of raucous laughter, Firestone insisted,

"That's the *only* way the old fool could get what he wants! He'll have to shoot me!"

"A dozen slugs on the bar gents," announced Gates, after a careful check of the cartridges. "Take your places and get set."

"We'll draw at your command, Gates," growled Firestone.

The old timers backed off from each other, their right hands hovering over their holstered revolvers. Little Jake dropped into a crouch, glowering ferociously, his grey-stubbled jaw out-thrust. Dan Firestone irritated him by

11

adopting a casual stance and yawning boredly.

When Gates called "Draw!", Firestone Colt cleared leather a full second faster than Little Jake's. Cursing explosively, Little Jake reholstered and crouched lower. He tried it again — and again — but it was painfully obvious Firestone's gunhand was the faster.

"Neither of 'em could stand up against a professional," Stretch mumbled with his mouth half-full. "They're slow, both of 'em."

"I know," nodded Larry. "But Little Jake's just a mite slower."

"All right, Firestone, you was too good for me this time," Little Jake conceded. "But I ain't through with you yet. I'll think of somethin' else."

"Some other time, Jake," chuckled Firestone, as they retrieved their shells and reloaded. "I got to be headed home now."

"Tell Norrie howdy from me," muttered Little Jake, fumbling with his cartridges. "How's she doin' anyway?"

"Doin' just fine," grunted Firestone. "Got a letter from the boy. Guess I forgot to mention. He'll be comin' home Friday week."

"Home from that fancy college, huh?" prodded Little Jake. "Young Mitch — home for keeps?"

"Home to stay and help run the old spread," nodded Firestone.

"Gotta say you're a lucky man," frowned Little Jake. "He's a real gentleman, that son of yours. High-educated and smart-talkin'."

"Not like you or me, Jake," said Firestone. "Well, that's education for you. It's what makes the difference between a gentleman and a no-account." He raised a hand in farewell and nodded to his hired hands. "Be seein' you, Jake."

As he moved away with four Hammerhead men in tow, the little man called after him.

"I'll be lookin' you up again, Dan, soon as I get back from Omaha."

"You do that," grinned Firestone.

13

"How about that?" Stretch remarked, while building himself another sandwich. "Seems they don't scrap *all* the time."

"They're neighbors, the barkeep said," Larry reminded him. "Neighbors have to get along. Or try to anyway."

He winced, barely resisting the impulse to clap hands to his ears. Little Jake was making an announcement, his booming voice causing the glassware to vibrate on the shelves behind the bar.

"All right you men — you heed me now! I didn't ride in just to wrassle with Dan Firestone! I'm here to hire herders . . . !"

"Forget it, Jake," jeered a local. "You got no hope of hirin' help in Hortonville."

"A man joins up with Double J," another remarked. "And, before he's had time to stow his gear in your bunkhouse, you're firin' him again."

"Don't you back-talk me, young feller!" chided Jake. "I could whup you one-handed!" He brandished his fists and scowled ferociously. "I can

14

whup any man in the house!"

"You tell 'em, Jake," sniggered the barfly in the far corner.

"Gosh sakes, Mister Jarvis," frowned Gates. "How're you *ever* gonna hire the help you need? Whole territory knows you got the meanest temper — you're the orneriest old heller in these parts. You've threatened to lynch men just for lookin' sideways at your daughter!"

"Tend your bar and mind your own blame business!" boomed Jake. He glared at the customers again. "I'll be drivin' three hunnerd head north to Omaha in the mornin'. Breed-stock for a new outfit up Dakota way. Don't plan on usin' my regular hands, so I'll hire three or more, pay forty and found if they last a month — not one thin dime if they quit on me."

"If that's your idea of a fair offer, it's no wonder you can't hire herders," gibed an aged townman.

"Hey, Jake, why don't you ask them strangers?" suggested the barfly. He hiccupped and pointed focusing blearily on the tall men seated in the opposite corner. "They look deadbeat, so maybe they're desperate. I mean — desperate enough to sign on with the proddiest jasper in all Nebrasky."

Little Jake turned to stare at the Texans. They munched their food and returned his stare with interest, as he trudged over to say his piece. In their almost two decades of drifting, many a man had sought to hire them. They were somewhat more versatile than the average frontiersman, having tried a variety of chores, everything from riding shotgun to railroading, from lumberjacking to prospecting. But their rig indicated they had been raised in cattle country. When their bankroll was thin, they were apt to accept almost any offer. Right now, they were financial to the tune of some $300. They could afford to refuse Jake Jarvis's proposition and were tempted to do just that, because the little fireball was bumptious, belligerent and abusive.

"Worked cattle before, haven't you?" he demanded.

"We're from Texas, old timer," drawled Stretch. "That's where cattle was invented."

"Don't call me 'old'!" shouted Jake. "I ain't so old I couldn't cut you down to size, you doggone stringbean!" He glowered over his shoulder at his grinning audience. "I can whup any man in the house!"

"Is this your regular way of hirin' help?" challenged Larry.

"I own my spread — that makes me the boss," growled Jake. "And that means I can talk any way I like."

"I'm waitin' to hear you talk," countered Larry. "Up till now, all I hear is hollerin' and bull-roarin'."

"Too rough for you, am I?" jeered Jake. "Why, sure! I've broke bigger men than you. Couple days on the trail with me, and you'd be beggin' for mercy. I don't need your kind. I can drive three hunnerd critters from here to Omaha with just my gal and

Kate and my chuck-boss."

"Two men and a girl — to push that many beeves?" Larry grinned scornfully.

"I wouldn't want to trust a couple no-account drifters anyway!" snapped Jake. "Seen your kind before. Around you, a decent gal like my Kate wouldn't be safe!"

"There he goes again," chuckled the aged townman.

"Hold your damn fool tongue, old Sidney!" roarerd Jake.

"Every time a stranger shows up, you figure he's gonna make a play for Kate," jeered the local.

"Little feller, you better remember we're from the South," Stretch grimly warned. "We don't talk fancy — and maybe we look like trail-trash — but we know how to behave around decent women." He frowned at the other drinkers, warning them against derisive comment. "We got chivalry."

"Prove it!" challenged Jake. "Ride for Double J for just one month, and *prove* I can trust you around Kate!"

"You and your big mouth," chided Larry, scowling at the bemused Stretch.

"Put up or shuddup!" taunted Jake.

"Hell, runt, we don't *have* to . . . " began Stretch.

"We don't have to, but we're gonna," declared Larry.

"Deal?" demanded Jake.

"Deal," said Larry.

"That's all." Jake gestured impatiently. "Get your butts outa them chairs and tag me. We're headed back to Double J rightaway."

"We'll be along," said Larry, "when we're through eatin'."

"I say *now*!" roared Jake.

"You heard what my buddy said," growled the taller Texan. "We'll be along when we're through eatin'." "And, if that don't set kindly with you," offered Larry, "go ahead and fire us."

"You don't get off *that* easy!" breathed Jake, retreating to the batwings. "I'll give you just two minutes, hear?"

19

He fished out a battered timepiece and squinted at it. "Two minutes! Not one second longer!" From the entrance, he glared defiantly at the grinning locals and loudly predicted, "I'll break them two smart-alecks! They won't last the month!"

"Now see what you done?" complained Stretch, after the little man had slammed out. "Now we gotta stick with that bull-roarin' old buzzard a whole month — just to prove we're as tough as him."

Quit your beefin'," grunted Larry, taking another pull at his beer. "Remember how it's been for us this past year? Every place we go, we run into strife, end up fightin' somebody else's fight. I'm weary of it."

"I'm as weary as you," shrugged Stretch.

"So, for just a month, we'll work as regular ranch-hands," said Larry. "Maybe that's what we need. I mean to get back to where we started, workin' for forty and found. That's what I call the quiet life, big feller." He finished his share of the cold cuts and corn bread, munching pensively. "Just ordinary, regular ranch chores."

"I gotta admit it sounds peaceful," Stretch conceded, "when I think of this past year. All the hard ridin', all the fightin'. Riskin' our necks all the time. I swear it gets monotonous."

"As for that sawed-off old heller," drawled Larry, nodding to the batwings. "We can handle him easy enough."

"I got a sneakin' hunch you admire him," muttered Stretch.

"You could be right about that," Larry agreed. "But don't ask me why. I haven't figured it out yet."

They finished eating and drinking. As they rose to their feet, Larry glanced at the clock atop the shelves and noted five minutes had passed since Little Jake's exit. Unhurriedly, he ambled across to the bar to buy a quart of rye. Gates accepted payment made change, then grinned at him and remarked,

"I never knew a ranch-hand that

enjoyed workin' for Little Jake."

"How about his regular help?" asked Larry.

"Just three of 'em," offered Gates. "They live at the spread — with their wives and kids. Jake trusts 'em around Miss Kate, on account of they got their own women to fret about — you know what I mean?" As the Texans started for the entrance he grinned affably and wished them well. "All the luck, gents."

"Gracias, amigo," nodded Larry. "We'll be seein' you."

"Little Jake was pacing beside the hitch-rail, his blood at boiling point, when the tall men emerged.

"Two minutes I said!" he raged, as they slipped their reins. "Hey, what's that you're totin'?"

"It's called rye," Larry patiently explained, as he stowed the bottle in his saddlebag. "We keep it for emergencies."

"Such as gettin' thirsty," said Stretch. "Now that's a *real* emergency."

"If you no-accounts think you're gonna drink your way from Double J to the Omaha loadin' pens . . . !" began Jake.

"Where's your horse, Boss?" asked Larry.

"I don't reckon he owns a horse," frowned Stretch. "Couldn't find a critter little enough for him to straddle, huh Boss? Well, that's okay. You can ride double with me."

"I don't trust jokers!" fumed Jake. "Every time you galoots open your mouths, you're back-talkin' me!"

"We'd best ride slow, big feller," Larry suggested. I mean, if he plans on runnin' all the way home, how's he gonna keep up with us?"

"Never was a horse I couldn't ride, damn and blast you!" roared Jake. He whirled and hurled a command, bellowing so loudly that citizens two blocks away heard him clearly. A stablehand emerged from a barn, leading a saddled charcoal.

"Comin', Mister Jarvis . . . !"

"Get a hustle on, consarn you!" yelled Jake. "Or, so help me, I'll break every bone in your no-good carcass!"

The stablehand, some twenty years Jake's junior and built like an ox, broke into an obedient run, hurrying to deliver the black, while the Texans traded amused grins. It seemed every citizen of Hortonville was completely intimidated by Double J's trigger-tempered owner — or at least pretending to be.

As he arrived, the stablehand aimed a wink at the strangers. Jake cursed luridly, lifted a boot, missed his stirrup and cursed again.

"Don't just stand there gawkin'!" he raged. "Gimme a boost!" Boosted astride by the stablehand, he jerked the black's head around and scowled at the Texans. "C'mon, you two! Get mounted!"

Out of Hortonville rode the Lone Star Hellions, after a visit so short as to leave no firm impression of the town on their minds. From a rise to the north they had studied it, but the distance had been considerable. Glancing back now, Larry decided Little Jake's hometown was pretty much a replica of a hundred-and-one cattle communities scattered across the western states.

"We'll give that burg a look-over," Stretch remarked, "when we get back from Omaha."

"Looks like a peaceable town," shrugged Larry.

Little Jake turned in his saddle to stare back at them and assert,

"It'll be plenty lively come Friday week, when Mitch Firestone arrives on the westbound stage. Whole Hammerhead crew'll be in to welcome him." He barked at them again. "Don't hold back, consarn you. Ride up level with me!" They heeled their animals. Larry brought his sorrel up to Jake's right side, while Stretch advanced his pinto to his left. "Texans, huh? You ain't told me your names yet."

"You didn't get around to askin'," drawled Larry. "He's Emerson. I'm Valentine."

"He's Larry. I'm Stretch," offered the taller Texan.

"I should've noticed before," Jake said suspiciously. "You bucks tote a helluva lotta hardware. Three six-shooters and two Winchesters. Listen, if you ain't nothin' better than owlhooters — on the run from the law — you'll get no protection from me. The sheriff of this here territory, Amos Trager, he's a friend of mine. Deputy Bloomfeld too."

"Good to know you got some friends hereabouts, old timer," grinned Larry. "The way you whoop and holler, we were thinkin' every citizen was your enemy."

"I got *no* enemies!" snapped Jake. "Ain't a man hereabouts with nerve enough to make *me* his enemy!"

"Now that you've got us scared stiff, why don't we talk about these critters we're drivin' to Omaha?" Stretch suggested. "Breed-stock, you said?"

"Consigned to the A-Bar ranch," muttered Jake. "That's a new outfit up in Creighton County, South Dakota.

We deliver 'em to the Omaha loadin' pens, help get 'em into boxcars. Railroad's responsibility from then on. Might be they'll need two trains. A-Bar's agent earmarked them breeders on my range. I got 'em bedded in my east quarter. I collect the cash in Omaha, and that's all you need to know."

"From here to Omaha — three hundred head," mused Stretch. "I calculate five of us could drive 'em there in a couple days."

"Four herders most of the way," said Jake. "Curly Becker, my chuck-boss, he'll be fetchin' his wagon along. Me and Kate and you two, we can handle the whole bunch. Easy route. Plenty grass and water. Less than fifty mile of good country." He squinted at them warily. "Bachelors, are you?"

"And we aim to stay that way," Larry assured him.

"That's what *you* say," retorted Jake. "You ain't seen my daughter Kate yet. Well, by jumpin' Judas, you better not get no fool notions. I've fired more skirt-chasin' no-accounts than I could keep count of, and all for the same damn reason."

"They tried to spark Miss Kate?" prodded Larry.

"And she ain't for the likes of them," growled Jake. "I'm savin' her, understand? She's gonna have herself a husband, sure, but he won't be no deadbeat cowpoke."

"Just so we'll know where we stand, old timer — " began Stretch.

"If your skinny sidekick calls me 'old' one more time," Jake warned Larry, "I'll start on him with my bare fists!"

"Now I savvy why every citizen hereabouts is a friend of yours — old timer," drawled Larry. "It's that gentle way you have of talkin' to folks."

"Sure, he's gentle," nodded Stretch. "Gentle as a cougar with a bullet-burned butt."

"What he'd say . . . ?" began Jake, his eyes agleam.

"He said take it easy," grinned Larry. "We'll treat Miss Kate respectful and friendly, and we won't try to spark her. We'll be — uh — like brothers to her. How about that?"

"Brothers you say?" jerked Jake. "If I'd had sons like you I swear I'd have shot myself from the shame of it."

"If you'd sired us, old timer, you wouldn't *need* to shoot yourself," countered Larry.

"On account of *we'd* shoot *you*," explained Stretch.

While Jake turned purple and searched his vocabulary for a suitable retort, Larry relentlessly declared.

"We'd call it an insult — gettin' sired by an old buzzard as ornery as you."

For another hundred yards of the east trail, the little fireball was burntout, speechless with indignation. Never had strangers dared back-talk him so scathingly — especially after being hired by him. What manner of saddletramps were these, he asked himself.

"Loco. Plain loco," he decided. "No

29

man with a brain in his head would talk that way to Jake Jarvis. But, so long as you savvy cattle, I'll let you work the whole month."

"You might's well," opined Larry. "Pushin' three hundred head to Omaha would be too big a chore for you and Miss Kate and a chuck-boss." A short time later, when Jake sank spur and hustled his mount off the trail, he called after him. "Where to now?"

"Up top of this here rise," replied Jake. "I have to take — another look at it."

"At what?" wondered Stretch. "It's near dark now. What can he see?"

"Let's find out," said Larry.

They followed the little man to the summit of the rise. From that vantage point, they scanned the verdant territory to the southeast, rolling green hills, vast stretches of graze separated by a line fence. Little Jake's stubbled face was suddenly solemn, wistful. They noted the yearning in his eyes as he pointed to the barely visible circle of water away to the south.

"You can just about see it if you look careful. That's it. That's the Glory Hole. And I'd give ten years of my life for just a half-share of it."

"Close by the line fence," observed Stretch.

"On Hammerhead land," sighed Jake.

"From here I see a creek," frowned Larry. "Looks to be runnin' clear across your range. I'd say you got water enough, so what d'you care about that one hole on Firestone's land?"

"You'd never savvy, Valentine," muttered Jake.

"Not unless you explain it," said Larry.

"I don't owe you no explanations," Jake retorted. "C'mon, let's ride. I crave my supper."

They reached the Double J headquarters in the first half-hour after sundown, a stoutly-constructed, double-storied ranch-house set back from the tangle of work corrals, the barn and the low-roofed bunkhouse. As they reined up and dismounted in front of the barn the little man frowned toward the other buildings, three sizeable cabins about which eight small children played, scampering around the vegetable plots and the chicken coops.

"Real family-type outfit," Stretch remarked, trading waves with the ranch-hands and their gingham-gowned wives. "Real friendly."

"This here's Valentine and Emerson!" Jake bellowed at his men. "Dunno how long they'll last. A mite too sassy for my likin'."

"You mean they got you sized up already, Jake?"

This challenge was aimed by the chuck-boss, a tall, stoop-shouldered veteran emerging from the cook-shack to appraise the new hands. Curly Becker's nickname was well-earned; his beard was as crinkly as his man greying mane. He grinned unconcernedly, when Jake barked at him.

"Don't start on me, Curly! Where's Kate?"

"In the house," said the chuck-boss, nodding to the Texans. "Howdy, boys."

The Texans returned his greeting, then turned to match stares with the young woman stepping out onto the ranch-house porch. In the light of the oil-lamps she was clearly visible, a healthy, boldly-contoured blonde, her thumbs hooked in a concho-studded belt, her shoulders squared. Studying her as he lifted his Stetson, Larry conceded the ex-employees of Double J had reason enough for trying to court her, for being smitten at their first glimpse of her. She stood like a man. Also she dressed as a man. Her cotton shirt was tucked into well-worn Levis that emphasized her rounded hips and shapely thighs. But, though the pose and rigout was masculine, Kate Jarvis was unmistakeably female, as evidenced by her generous bosom, the hair hanging about her shoulders in

33

lustrous abandon and the smile that lit her beautiful face, causing the blue eyes to sparkle.

"Well, howdy there," she called.

"Kate, I already warned these jaspers . . . !" began Jake.

"Right proud to meet you, Miss Kate," nodded Stretch. "I'm Stretch and this here's my partner. You can call him Larry."

"And, just so your hot-headed pappy don't get no wrong notions, we ain't here to court you," grinned Larry. "We like you fine, Miss Kate, but we ain't the marryin' kind."

"I like you too — the both of you," she cheerfully declared.

"Hold on now! This ain't no way for . . . !" blustered Jake.

"Don't mind Pa," offered Kate. "He's leery of every new hand, every stranger that happens by."

"We noticed," said Larry.

"Consarn you, Kate . . . !"gasped Jake.

"Quit your hollerin' and come get

your supper," she ordered. "Larry — Stretch — you hungry? Curly'll take care of you after you've stabled your animals and stowed your gear in the bunkhouse."

"Much obliged, Miss Kate," nodded Stretch.

"In vain, Jake Jarvis harangued the Texans, his daughter, the chuck-boss, his hired hands and their families. It seemed those who knew him best were least affected by his fury. He raged and ranted, while Larry and Stretch stabled their horses, stowed their gear and socialized with the other hands. Not until he had yelled himself breathless did he give up and trudge into the house for his supper.

In Omaha, that night, the agent of the A-Bar ranch relaxed in a hotel in sight of the railroad depot, the purchase price of the breed herd safely locked away in the vault of the Pioneer Bank.

And, in the busy centre of the big town, a well-known panhandler was being thrown out of a saloon. The lean, handsomely-tailored young man known hereabouts as English Eddie gasped protests that fell on deaf ears and suffered the indignity of a swift kick from the bouncer. Watched by locals laughing derisively, he plummeted from the saloon porch to collapse in the street, a dandy with dirt on his fine clothes, a dude with few friends in Nebraska's biggest city.

"Last warnin', Eddie!" growled the bouncer. "Next time you try beggin' in here, I'll work you over with my fists — and then you won't look so all-fired purty."

"I was not begging." The panhandler picked himself up, retrieved his derby and frowned reproachfully at his assailant. "I was trying to arrange a loan — "

"You're the most comical deadbeat I ever knew — I'll say that much for you," gibed the bouncer, while the onlookers chuckled heartily. "Always good for a laugh."

"When my next remittance arrives — from the estate of my family in Suffolk — that's in England you know . . . " began the pandhandler.

"Vamoose!" scowled the bouncer.

Edward Giles Roderick shrugged resignedly, turned away and began walking uptown toward another saloon, the Coronado. Irresponsible and shiftless, he rarely spared a thought for his future. The Omaha lawmen and the gambling fraternity held him in contempt, regarding him as a no-talent misfit, a foreigner out of his element, a too-enthusiastic toper and an inept gambler.

But people can change, as this seemingly useless aristocrat would soon learn. Fickle Fate was taking a hand in his fortunes. He would be manipulated by forces beyond his control and thrown into strange company.

Company with a Texas accent.

2

Cue to Exit

THE dandy entered the Coronado and strode purposefully across the crowded barroom, making for the stairs and trying to ignore the grins aimed at him by the customers, the burly barkeeps and the cigar-puffing tablehands.

'Barbarians, all of them,' he reflected. 'Why do they deride me? Confound it, my wife owns this place. The least they could do is show respect.'

As he climbed the stairs he indulged in self-sympathy. A few months ago, marrying Melva Kiley had seemed a great idea, an inspiration in fact. The beautiful answer to his problem of near-penury. Melva *was* beautiful. More important, she was enterprising and a shrewd businesswoman. She owned the Coronado, a thriving concern which, in time, could become the most profitable gambling house in all of Omaha. Even more important was the fact that he had fallen in love for the first time in his life. He had wooed Melva as a lady of quality should be wooed and, for the first weeks of their marriage, had happily considered himself the luckiest man alive. But that happiness had been short-lived; it was painfully obvious Melva was bored with him. Returning to their private quarters some time ago, he found that his few personal effects had been moved to a smaller bedroom, the last room along the gallery. When it came to making a point, Melva was nothing if not explicit.

He knocked gently at the door of her office, still intimidated by the beauty who had spurned him.

"Who?" she called.

"Edward — your husband," he replied.

"Don't bother me now," she chided.

"Tell Big Benny I said give you a bottle — and stay away from me."

He squared his shoulders, turned the knob and thrust the door open.

"Now, see here, my dear," he began, as he strode into the room. "This won't do you know. It simply isn't good enough — "

He came to an abrupt halt, frowning uncertainly at his wife and her companion. Melva, dark-haired and slender, garbed in a shimmering gown of green silk, perched on the edge of the mahogany-topped desk with her shapely legs crossed. She patted at her raven tresses and smiled brazenly at Gus Millane, the pomaded, sardonic gambler who acted as her manager. He lounged on the sofa in his shirtsleeves, nursing a drink, returning her smile and insolently ignoring her perplexed spouse.

Roderick, in his confusion and anger, resorted to sarcasm.

"I trust I'm not intruding?"

"Ed, why don't you just shut up and

get out of here?" suggested Millane, without deigning to look at him.

"Far as I'm concerned, you've been intruding ever since I made the fool mistake of marrying you," drawled Melva.

"My dear, it's obvious we need to discuss our situation," said Roderick. "But — if you please — not in front of an employee. I have my standards after all."

"Standards — you?" she jeered. "Who do you think you're foolin? I'll admit I fell for your spiel, all that high class charm of yours, the English accent and all, but I should've known you'd never change."

"Once a deadbeat, always a deadbeat," muttered Millane.

"All that fine talk of how you met Queen Victoria," said Melva. "And the grand balls in the family castle . . . "

"All true, I assure you," declared Roderick.

"Crazy lies," she accused. "Oh, sure. You're English. But I wouldn't call you high class, Ed. You admitted what you were, and I should've realized what it meant. A remittance man. They send cash once in a while, your relatives . . . "

"Booze money," gibed Millane. "Nickels and dimes."

"If your people were all that rich, they'd have sent more," opined Melva. "Why would a rich man's son have to beg booze in every Omaha bar? It doesn't add up, Ed. Admit it. Your people aren't rich. My guess is they own a store in some cheap corner of London. You got into a jam and they had to send you out of the country."

"My father was never a merchant," Roderick protested. "He's a baronet. Extremely wealthy, I assure you. The estate — vast areas of Suffolk — has been a family possession for five generations of Rodericks . . . "

"He tells it smooth," grinned Millane. "Same speech he gives the suckers, when he's angling for a handout."

"I'm tired of carrying him," Melva said curtly.

"You have to understand," said Roderick. "My father *could* increase my allowance, but he stubbornly refuses, insisting, I should learn to survive on the pittance he sends me."

"I've heard it all before, Ed, and I'm not convinced," said Melva. "When I married you, I thought you'd shape up, get wise to yourself and help run this business. But hard work and you are old enemies. You're useless as a tablehand and too high-and-mighty to tend bar . . . "

"Would you reduce me to such menial chores?" he challenged.

"He doesn't catch on fast, does he?" Millane remarked to the woman. "Better get used to the idea, Ed. You're all through."

"I — beg your pardon . . . ?" gasped Roderick.

"And it's a mite late for beg pardons," drawled Millane. "You had your chance and bungled it."

43

"We speak the same language, Gus and I," said Melva. "I'm still full owner of the Coronado. At the start, I thought of dealing you in, but now I realize that would've been a bad mistake. So I'm inviting you to move out. Gus is gonna be my partner . . ." Again that brazen smile. Roderick's scalp crawled, as she winked at the grinning gambler and added, "In more ways than one."

"Have you no shame, Melva?" he chided.

Millane guffawed and slapped his knee, while the dark-haired beauty eyed her husband with grim amusement and drawled a taunt.

"You sound like a play-actor in some two-bit tent show." Millane guffawed again as she mimicked the abashed Roderick. "Have you no shame, Melva? Heaven help you, Ed. You're a pitiful excuse for a man, and that's putting it mild. You know about Gus and me. You know what's been going on behind your back . . ."

"Not until this moment," breathed Roderick.

"And what can you do about it?" she coldly challenged. "If you were half a man, you'd want to beat his brains out!"

"Let him try," muttered Millane.

"I've no talent for fisticuffs." Roderick sighed heavily and turned toward the door. "I realize, of course, that a violent reaction is considered normal in this primitive society, this notorious Wild West. You'd probably enjoy seeing your paramour beat me senseless."

"I'll give you a few days to get used to the idea," said Melva. "We'll make it just three days, Ed, and then I'll expect you to move out. That clear enough for you? Three days. Find yourself a job . . ."

"A job. Him?" Millane chuckled scathingly. "That's funny. What could he *do*? He's no use to anybody — including himself."

Shocked to the core, the Englishman moved out to the gallery. Millane finished his drink, got up and ambled across to shove the door shut, then grinned reassuringly at the woman.

"We sure don't need him, Melva honey. Even as a swamper, swabbing spittoons, he wouldn't be worth his pay."

"Tell me something I don't know," she shrugged. "It was my mistake."

"We'll do fine together, you and me," he predicted. "I know how to operate a gambling set-up — and make sure it pays off big. Inside a year we'll be rich enough to shake the dust of Nebraska off our clothes and go settle in a *real* city. New York — Chicago — you name it."

"Let's not forget our competition," she frowned, moving around to seat herself behind the desk. "McDonald's Queen of Diamonds and Lamont's Crystal Casino. They're big, and getting bigger. Seems some new joy-house is starting up every week. Making our fortune from the Coronado might take longer than you say."

"You just leave all the planning to me," he offered. "I got it all figured out."

"I'll be counting on you," she murmured. Again she patted at her hair and smiled her sensual smile. "So far you're doing fine, Gus. You're ten times the man poor Ed could ever hope to be." As he made to open the door, she chuckled softly. "Don't forget your coat, lover."

★ ★ ★

In the hour after sun-up, when the Texans straddled Double J cow-ponies and began pushing the breed-herd north, they had every reason to anticipate an easy run. Well-fed and placid, these critters weren't about to give trouble. Little Jake, riding point and gesticulating impatiently, bellowing unnecessary commands, was the only influence apt to startle the herd. Kate, still rigged in male attire, rode flank and traded cheerful waves with the new hands. Her blonde hair was piled atop her head and held in place by a battered Stetson. A cartridge-belt girded her trim waist, the butt of a Colt jutting from its holster. Curly Becker brought his wagon up and around the moving cattle to take the lead, while the Texans headed off a few bunch-quitters and swapped comments.

"Talks like a man — rides like a man," Stretch remarked.

"But never say she *looks* like a man," grinned Larry.

"Not if you're in front of her," shrugged the taller Texan. "But get in back of her, watch her hustlin' that gelding of hers, and you could think you were seein' a regular cowpoke."

"Plenty water and graze 'tween here and Omaha, Jake says," drawled Larry. "The goin' will be easy, big feller. Not like some of those other drives we've worked. Remember the old Chisholm Trail?"

"I remember it good," nodded Stretch. "But I'd as soon forget it."

The 300 plodded north at a steady pace, tagging the chuck-wagon to the downswing of the Platte's great bend. There were no mishaps, when Little Jake and his new hands hustled them into the shallows, making their crossing less than 25 miles from the junction of the Platte and the broad Missouri. The only animal breaking from the column in midstream was retrieved by Kate, with skill of which any veteran herder would have been proud; she swam her gelding after the bawling calf, twirled her rope and neatly dropped her loop over the tossing head, then guided him back to the main bunch.

Again the Texans were moved to comment.

"I couldn't of handled that any slicker," complained Stretch. "And it just don't seem right."

"She'd look better in skirts," opined Larry. "Drivin' cattle is no chore for a female."

The noon stop was brief. Curly got a fire going, but only long enough to boil up a pot of coffee. At Little Jake's insistence, they ate cold tack, washed it down with black coffee and were into their saddles again by the time Curly was killing the fire.

"This way, we make the big hollow by sundown," the chuck-boss explained. "Best place you ever saw for a night-camp. A good spring and plenty feed. Easy to bed the herd and keep 'em bedded."

"One nighthawk's enough, huh Curly?" prodded Stretch.

"Just one of us ridin' the rim of the hollow," nodded Curly. "We've traveled this route many a time. If you're pushin' five hundred or more, a couple nighthawks is all we need. For a herd this size, one is plenty."

In the last quarter-hour before the setting of the sun, the wagon was stalled in a grove a short distance from the basin rim. Running the herd down to its green floor was an easy chore; Jake, his daughter and the Texans had the three hundred bedded by full dark.

It was the first time Larry and Stretch had heard the little rancher express satisfaction — about anything.

"Best night-camp in all of east Nebrasky, this here holler," he drawled, as they began to climb to where Curly was starting his cook-fire. "When I deliver beef to Omaha, it's always in prime condition. That's what I told A-Bar's agent, after he earmarked these critters. 'They'll look just as healthy in the loadin' pens,' I told him, 'as they looked on home range.' I'm a man that looks to the future."

"Why, sure," nodded Larry. "A smart cattleman has to think ahead."

"Years ahead," declared Jake. "When we built our spreads in Horton County, me and Dan Firestone and all them other ranchers, we all had the same notion. We knew Omaha was close, with plenty good land in between. Never no long drives. Never pushin' a herd near loco from thirst. We drive 'em steady and they get all the water and feed they need so, when them

51

buyers look'em over, why, they ain't sweated off a pound, not one pound." He leaned forward as they finished their climb, his nostrils flaring. "Hope Curly's keepin' his stewpot full. I swear I could eat double my share."

"Pa's got the biggest appetite in Horton County," smiled Kate.

"Never you mind how much I eat, gal," growled Jake. "You got more important things to be thinkin' on. Near twenty years old you are. High time you was wed and settled down."

The Texans learned more of Jake Jarvis's plan for his daughter's future while smoking their after-supper cigarettes and listening to Curly Becker. The Double J boss had elected to make a circuit of the basin before turning in. Kate toted a towel and soap to a spring some eighty yards east. As soon as father and daughter were out of earshot, the chuck-boss relaxed and began swapping confidences with the new hands. Did they intend working the whole month? Larry assured him they would do so, if only out of sheer cussedness, if only to prove they could take as much sass as Little Jake could hurl at them, and retaliate in kind.

"He was always this way," Curly assured them. "After a time, you get used to his wild temper and his hollerin'." He lit his corncob pipe with a twig drawn from the fire, puffed pensively and offered a prediction. "He'll cool down some. He'll feel a sight easier in his mind, if his plans for Kate work out."

"You mean her gettin' wed?" prodded Stretch.

"To Mitch Firestone, old Dan's boy," muttered Curly. "Nobody else'll do. It just has to be young Mitch — him with all his book-learnin' and his fine manners."

"How does Kate feel about young Mitch?" asked Larry.

"Well, I guess she's always had a hankerin' for him," shrugged Curly. "But Dan and Norrie Firestone, they're lookin' for Mitch to get himself a real high-class bride. A lady, you know what I mean? Quality. A high education, just like Mitch hisself." He grinned secretively. "Well, if Jake has his way, Kate'll be the only gal for Mitch."

"It ain't for us to say, Curly," frowned Stretch. "But Kate'd have to change some. I mean — uh — a young feller like this Mitch, educated and all, he's apt to shy clear of a gal that rides astride and works and talks like a forty-a-month cowpoke."

"Jake already thought of that," said Curly. "In Omaha, he'll be lookin' around, lookin' to hire some kinda teacher, like a chaperone, you know? Maybe a schoolma'am."

"Private lessons for Kate?" frowned Larry.

"Somebody who'll teach her how to act like a high-born lady?" challenged Stretch. "Well now . . . " He dribbled smoke through his nostrils and nodded thoughtfully, "maybe that's a fair enough idea."

"It could work," mused Larry.

"Sure it'll work," declared Curly. "She's rough and tough, but she ain't ignorant. Didn't quit county school till she was fifteen years old. Oh, sure. She can read and write and figure. It's just — well — there was always ranch chores for her. Jake got into the habit of usin' her like she was one of the hired hands. But now he's smarter. Now he savvies it was a mistake, treatin' her like a cowpoke. And he aims to make up for it." He puffed at his pipe and chuckled softly. "He couldn't buy the Glory Hole from Firestone, couldn't win it from him in any kind of gamble, so he figures this is the only way. He'll settle for a half share of that damn pond, he says."

"So *that's* what he's aimin' for?" Larry grinned wryly, "Takin' a heap for granted I'd say."

"He's been goin' off at half-cock all his life," drawled Curly. "Too old to change now. The way he sees it, Dan just couldn't refuse him."

"If Kate got to be Mrs Mitch

Firestone," said Larry.

"Be like keepin' it in the family, he says," grinned Curly.

"We still don't savvy why it means so much to him — that one damn waterhole," said Stretch.

"You wouldn't believe he's sentimental, would you now?" asked Curly.

"That's right," nodded Stretch. "We'd *never* believe he's sentimental."

The chuck-boss stared away toward the basin-rim, listening intently. Though he heard no hoofbeats, no indication his boss was returning, he dropped his voice almost to a whisper.

"Jake'd nail my hide to the barn wall if he knew I'd told you, so you keep it under your hats, understand?"

"Don't worry on our account," muttered Larry. "We ain't apt to gab about it."

"The Glory Hole is where Jake used to take her," Curly confided. "Who?" demanded Stretch.

"Annie May," said Curly. "Kate's ma. Back when he was courtin' her.

Buggy rides in the moonlight, you know? But that was way back before the land agent brought a surveyor in to check all the boundaries. Wasn't no fences then, and Jake was takin' a heap for granted, just like always. He figured the Glory Hole was on *his* land, only it turned out it *wasn't*"

"Part of Hammerhead range," guessed Stretch.

"Damn right," nodded Curly. "And, years later, after Jake and Annie May'd been wed a couple years, she gave birth to Kate. One more year was all Annie May had. Some kind of fever. Doc Dudley did all he could for her, but it wasn't no use. You likely noticed the grave on the hill back of the house."

"That's another reason Kate was raised like a boy," Larry realized. "No mother to teach her things."

"Every time Jake rides by that waterhole — or even *thinks* of it — he gets to rememberin' Annie May," said Curly. "Talked to me about it, just once. 'It's like a debt,' he said. 'Like

57

somethin' I owe Annie May.' He wants that doggone hole should stay in the family, says he'd settle for half-share of it."

"I sure wish him luck," frowned Larry.

"Me too," grunted Stretch. "But, if you ask me, I'd say it's gonna be quite a chore. Nothin' personal against Miss Kate. But teachin' her to act like a high-class lady . . . " He shook his head dubiously, "that's gonna be quite a chore."

★ ★ ★

It was 2 p.m., the August air crisp and bracing, when Little Jake and his helpers drove the 300 over the last quarter-mile south of the Omaha railroad depot and the network of corrals beside the steel tracks. A-Bar's agent was on hand to welcome them, to look the herd over and express his satisfaction.

"Every animal in good condition,

Jarvis, just as you promised," he acknowledged, as they shook hands.

"Double J always deals square," Jake grimly asserted. "I'll whup the man says otherwise — with . . ."

"One hand tied behind your back," interjected Stretch, winking at the agent.

"Quit sassin' me and go tend the horses!" barked Jake.

"If you're ready, we'll go along to the bank now," offered the agent. "Depot crew's about ready to load the stock into the box cars. We'll have completed the transaction by the time the northbound's ready to roll."

"Can't be too soon for me," growled Jake. "I got other business to tend 'fore we start for home." He barked at the Texans again. "We'll be movin' south again — nine o'clock tonight. And that means nine sharp. Nary a minute later — hear?"

"You and me gonna eat at that same hotel, Pa?" asked Kate. "The Lembeck House?"

"Around seven o'clock," nodded Jake. "Meantime, you come along with me and Mister Richards. Can't afford to turn you loose in this town. Always some smart-aleck tryin' to spark you." As he took her arm and began moving after the agent, he scowled over his shoulder at Curly and the Texans and bellowed a reminder. "You meet us back here by the wagon. *Sober*, savvy?"

"Nine sharp, old timer," grinned Larry. "We'll be seein' you."

"I'll be here," Curly assured the Texans. "but, 'tween now and then, I'll be visitin' with my Cousin Luke. Hey, you boys been in Omaha before?"

"A time or two," said Larry.

"Safest saloon is the Yerby Bar," offered Curly. "Good booze and an even break at the games of chance. Leastways that's how it was, last time we were here."

Until sundown, Little Jake and his daughter combed the big town in a futile search for a private tutor, a

60

schoolteacher willing to spend some ten days at Double J or maybe a refined widow of gentle background or the wife of some Omaha clergyman. Jake's quest seemed doomed to failure, mainly because he had never learned the art of the soft approach, the polite tactful overture. He never asked; he challenged. He never requested; he demanded.

"What's the matter with all these dang-blasted respectable folks?" he wondered, as he began steering Kate toward the Lembeck House. "I tell it plain enough, don't I? How come they won't listen?"

"Its like I've been tellin' you for years," said Kate. "No use hollerin' — not when you're askin' a favor."

"I *wasn't* hollerin', consarn you!"

"If you didn't holler, how come they covered their ears?"

"There has to be *somebody*. I had it all figured. Wasn't gonna leave Omaha without a special teacher to set you right. You need to get your rough

61

edges smoothed, child. That's what it takes to win a regular educated gent like young Mitch. You gotta be smooth and gentle and soft — like a real high-born lady."

"I swear I'm ready to do my darnedest," Kate wistfully assured her sire. "It'd be worth all the trouble."

"Got a hankerin' for Mitch, huh? " he prodded. "Well, that's as it oughta be. You keep right on hankerin', hear? If I catch you lookin' sideways at any other man . . . "

"You don't need to fret about that," declared Kate. "You know how I've always felt about Mitch."

"He'll feel that same way about you," Jake promised. "But not 'less'n we get you purtied up and female-ised, not 'less'n you learn how to be a lady."

At Yerby's Bar, Larry and Stretch were socializing with a percentage-girl, paying for her gin and listening to her tale of woe, listening patiently and somewhat wistfully, because this bulky and overpainted redhead was unmistakably a fellow-expatriate.

"Trouble with Omaha, and all the other big towns I've worked . . ." Her ample bosom rose and fell, as she heaved a sigh and swigged her third refill. "I'll tell you what the trouble is. Ain't enough Texans. That's what the trouble is."

Stretch took a stiff pull at his whiskey and nodded sympathetically.

"That's how we find it every place we go," he drawled. "Same thing all over. Not enough Texans."

"And the badge-toters hereabouts," she complained. "Mean hombres, all of 'em. Do-gooders. Killjoys. And the tinhorns and panhandlers ain't much better. Slim pickin's for the likes of me." She gestured wearily. "Like that one, for instance. Looks high class, don't he? A real big spender? Not a chance. A deadbeat. Talks like a gentleman. But just another two-bit panhandler."

Without great interest, the Texans

switched their gaze to the well-dressed local making a pitch to a visiting cattle-buyer. Edward Roderick, penniless and desperately thirsty, was trying to organize a loan.

"Just a temporary embarrassment, I assure you," he told the out-of-towner. "I expect to receive a substantial remittance from my connections in the old country. A day — two days at most. You'll be repaid, with interest if you wish . . . "

The cattle-buyer could not be conned. He edged away from Roderick, while the Texans eyed him scathingly and traded comments.

"Healthy, good-lookin' hombre like him," muttered Stretch. "You'd think he'd have more pride, wouldn't you now?"

"An honest day's work'd likely break his heart," scowled Larry.

"English Eddie, we call him," said the percenter. "Married Melva Kiley a little while back. I guess he figured he was onto a good thing, hitchin' up with

64

a saloonkeeper. Last I heard, she was gettin' ready to throw him out. Well, I sure don't blame her." She chuckled softly. "Hey, you oughta hear his pitch. He's some talker — gotta hand it to him. Claims he's kin to a genuine baronet. Sir Nigel Roderick of Suffolk, if you please! Ain't that somethin'?"

"I call it pitiful," Stretch said in disgust.

"You meet one panhandler, you've met 'em all," shrugged Larry.

"A few moments later, the Texans heard a shouted accusation that indicated English Eddie was in trouble. Again they turned to stare toward the bar. The Englishman was backing away from an irate towner, a red-faced jasper who swung a wild blow at him, missed and over-balanced against a table.

"Lousy, good-for-nothin' sneak-thief!" he bellowed. "Damn him to hell — he picked my pocket!"

"I assure you, my dear fellow, you're mistaken — you do me an injustice," protested Roderick.

"He got my wallet! raged the local. "He bumped against me and — when I felt for my wallet — it was gone!"

"That's Jimmy Geech," offered the redhead. "Got a mean temper when he's drunk. Worse when he's sober."

"Somebody ought to stop Geech before he . . . " began Larry.

He left the sentence unfinished. Geech's swift action took everybody by surprise, including the startled barkeep and a badly scared Roderick. With surprising agility, the towner vaulted the bar, shoved the barkeep aside and reached under the counter for his double-barreled shotgun.

"Now — you thievin' polecat . . . !" he roared, as the staff and customers began a wild scatter. "I'm gonna blow you apart — and you'll never rob another honest citizen!"

In fear for his life, the Englishman took to his heels. Geech loosed another wild yell, vaulted the counter again and took off in hot pursuit, still hefting the shotgun.

"Damn fool," growled Larry, leaping to his feet. "That cannon's cocked . . . !"

"Both barrels," nodded Stretch. "I noticed."

"What d'you care?" challenged the percenter, as they made for the batwings. "What if Geech blows a hole through the pandhandler? He'd be doin' him a favor."

But, despite their contempt for English Eddie, the Texans dashed out of Yerby's and pursued Geech and his intended victim. They had a healthy respect for the destructive force of a double charge of buckshot. Moreover the street was busy, a lot of locals out and about. If Geech cut loose, innocent parties might be injured — or worse. Spurred by their altruistic instincts, they hustled after the still-yelling Geech.

Roderick, almost out of breath, darted a worried glance backward and decided he should get off the street. He turned and made for the nearest doorway, the entrance to the Lembeck House.

When he barged into the lobby, Geech was close behind; he knew this for sure, because his pursuer's boots sounded loud and ominous on the hotel porch. Desperate, in panic, he stumbled toward the reception desk and the two people talking to the night-clerk.

"Young man — I beg you . . . !" he gasped. "Help me! I'm unarmed — and he's a homicidal maniac!"

Kate Jarvis was more humiliated than angered, when the Englishman scuttled around behind her, shielding himself against the infuriated Geech. For the first time, a stranger had failed to notice her pretty face. For the first time, a stranger had taken her for a man. And it rankled.

Sighting Geech and the leveled shotgun, the clerk loosed a wail of fear and disappeared under his desk. Little Jake stood his ground, bellowing a reprimand, while Geech yelled at Kate.

"Move away from that sneakin'

polecat — or you'll get it too, young feller!"

"Next galoot calls me young feller, I'm gonna bust his jaw!" cried Kate.

"I said *move away* . . . !" began Geech.

Abruptly and violently, Larry and Stretch arrived. At their heels was a local peace officer, a burly deputy brandishing a six-shooter.

"Stand aside — *I'll* take care of this . . . !" he yelled.

But, with that formidable weapon leveled at Kate and her father, the Texans weren't about to wait for the law to take over. They handled Geech in their own rough but efficient way. Stretch swung a leg at the backs of Geech's knees, causing him to slump backward, while Larry grabbed for the shotgun's barrels and forced the weapon upward. Geech's hand jerked and, with a deafening roar, the shotgun discharged, peppering the ceiling with shot.

"Let go of it now, you blame fool,"

growled Larry, "or I'll wrap it round your damn-blasted head!"

He wrenched the weapon from Geech's grasp. Geech mumbled something unintelligible, as Stretch gripped him by his coat-collar and jerked him upright.

"What was that you said?" demanded the deputy, glowering at him.

"I said — uh — I just remembered," frowned Geech.

"Just remembered what?" challenged the deputy.

"I'm awfully sorry." Geech shrugged apologetically and kept his gaze on the floor, too embarrassed to meet their eyes. "I just remembered — I left my wallet in my other coat."

3

The Truth About English Eddie

JIMMY GEECH'S announcement, somewhat of an anti-climax, won a mixed reaction. The only man laughing was Stretch; apparently nobody else saw the funny side of it. Whooping and chuckling, he stumbled across the lobby to flop into a chair.

"If that don't beat all!" he gasped.

Larry's ire hadn't cooled. He hefted the shotgun and, for a moment, the deputy was sure he would aim its stock at Geech's head. Little Jake was gesticulating angrily and bellowing a challenge.

"What kinda law enforcement d'you call this? A durn jackass bargin' in here with a cocked scattergun . . . !"

"Easy, old timer . . . " began the deputy.

"Don't you call me old!" stormed

Jake. "I could whup you with one hand tied behind of me — even if I was ninety years old! I can lick . . . !"

"He can lick any man in the house," grinned Stretch. "If you don't believe it, just ask Jake."

"You butt outa this!" barked Jake.

"Is it — all over . . . ?" asked the clerk, raising his head gingerly.

"It's all over, Carney," growled the deputy, seizing Geech's right arm. "I'm takin' this proddy fool to the lockup — give him time to cool off."

"I'm awful sorry . . . " began Geech.

"Under the circumstances, an apology hardly seems adequate," chided Roderick. Now that the danger had passed, he stepped clear of Kate and adjusted his cravat; he was striving to retrieve his dignity. "The man's a menace, officer. He had the audacity, the unbridled impudence, to accuse me of picking his pocket . . . "

"All right, Eddie, all right," scowled the deputy. "Don't make a speech. I'm not in the mood."

"The damage!" fretted the clerk. "Look at the ceiling!"

"Tell your boss he'll collect from Geech." The deputy shook his prisoner roughly. "Right, Geech?"

"I'll make it good," Geech promised. "Awful sorry for all the trouble I caused."

"Wait till Sheriff McVie hears about this," said the deputy. "By golly, Geech, you'll rue the day you went wild with a shotgun in Omaha." As he hustled his prisoner toward the entrance, he retrieved the shotgun from Larry and eyed him curiously. "You and your buddy are what I'd call fast on your feet."

"Had to be," Larry said gruffly. "He was totin' that cannon cocked. Might've hurt somebody."

Sure enough," agreed the deputy. "Well, thanks for the helpin' hand."

After the lawman had taken Geech away, Roderick subjected Kate to a bemused scrutiny and doffed his derby.

"My apologies, madam," he offered.

"I trust you'll excuse my error. No offense intended, I assure you."

"Yeah, okay," she shrugged. "No offense taken."

"I'm a stranger in a strange land," said Roderick, "constantly confused by the ways of frontier folk. Your attire, if you'll forgive my remarking, is somewhat unconventional. I never saw a lady — er — in male clothing . . ."

"She's female, and I oughta know," growled Jake, "on account of I'm her pa."

"My compliments, sir." Roderick accorded him a courteous bow. "I'm sure you're proud to be the father of so beautiful a young lady. And now, if you'll excuse me . . ."

He made to turn away, then winced apprehensively; Jake had seized his arm in a vice-like grip and was studying him intently, his eyes agleam.

"Hold on a minute, mister! I ain't through with you!"

"For gosh sakes, Jake," protested Stretch. "If you're thinkin' what I think you're thinkin' . . . "

"Valentine, tell your skinny sidekick to keep his fool mouth shut," Jake warned.

"Don't do nothin' rash," frowned Larry.

"Better heed your partner, Emerson," growled Jake.

"I wasn't talkin' to Stretch," said Larry. "I mean *you*, Jake. You're about to make a bad mistake."

"How come every sonofagun thinks he can read my mind?" raged Jake. He turned red and shook his fists, startling Roderick. "Consarn you, Valentine! When I need your advice . . . !"

"He's a deadbeat," Larry said bluntly. "If you got some idea of hirin' him — for anything — you'd better think twice."

"I resent the term 'deadbeat' and its implication," declared Roderick. "You have the advantage of me, sir . . . "

"Don't call me 'sir'," countered Larry. "Comin' from you, it sounds like a bad joke."

"Panhandlers is trouble, Jake," muttered Stretch. "You ought to know better."

"I don't care if he's a three-legged Chinaman!" asserted Jake, pounding the counter, causing the clerk to flinch from him. "Just so long as he's educated!"

"Educated?" Roderick drew himself up proudly. "Sir, I'll have you know I was sent down from Cambridge."

"That's good enough for me," said Jake. "Valentine, Emerson, you get outa here — and I mean *now*! I'll see you later! Meantime, I don't want no more of your doggone back-talk!"

"But . . ." began Stretch.

"Let the old fire-eater make his own mistakes," shrugged Larry, turning to the entrance. "And maybe he'll learn from 'em."

After the Texans had gone their way, Jake squinted up at the Englishman and asked,

"You had your supper yet?" Roderick shook his head. "All right, you come along and eat with Kate and me. I got a job for you, Mister — Whatever-You-Call-Yourself."

"My name is Edward Giles Roderick. I am the second son of Sir Nigel Roderick of Castle Roderick — that's in Suffolk you know." Roderick nodded affably to the little man. "Suffolk — England?"

"Yeah, sure," grunted Jake. "You say you're English. That's fine by me."

"And I am not, as your employees described me, a panhandler," said Roderick. "Whatever *that* means."

"Means a deadbeat," offered Kate. "Somebody beggin' for handouts."

"A beggar? Perish the thought!" frowned Roderick. "However, I do admit to a certain — er — financial embarrassment. If, therefore, your father wishes to employ me . . . "

"I reckon it's a chore you could handle, Roderick," said Jake. "C'mon, let's go eat and talk it over."

Over supper in the dining room of the Lembeck House, the Englishman listened to Jake's plan for his daughter's transformation from tomboy ranch-hand to lady of quality. He was at first incredulous. He was also hungry, so he lent an attentive ear to the little man's proposition, pensively studying the shy-grinning Kate, trying to assess her potential, asking himself the all-important question — was Jake Jarvis's notion so far-fetched? Was it possible this unrefined beauty could be trained, remolded, schooled in the social graces in so short a time?

"Astounding," he said softly, when Jake had finished.

"You gonna tell me I'm crazy — askin' too much?" challenged Jake.

"Don't holler, Pa," chided Kate. "You'll faze the other guests."

"Mister Jarvis, I approve your concern for the young lady's welfare," Roderick assured Jake. "And I've no doubt you have her best interests at heart — along with your interest in acquiring a certain waterhole . . . "

"It all ties in," muttered Jake. "She'd

be happy with young Mitch. I know he'd treat her right — and I reckon his pa'd do right by me. That's what I'm countin' on, Roderick. Up till now, me and Dan are just neighbors. But, if his Mitch ties up with my Kate, we'll be like kin. Anything Dan wants from me, he's welcome. Anything I want from him — how can he say 'no'?"

"I was about to say . . . " began Roderick.

"He's about to say it can't be done," sighed Kate.

"But it *can* be done. People can change. You're young, alert, intelligent. Given time, I believe I could tutor you, teach you the things you need to know, correct speech, good grooming and so forth."

"So . . . ?" prodded Jake.

"I want to be absolutely honest with you, sir," said Roderick. "I could certainly use the fee you offer . . . "

"Two hundred dollars — cash — when the job's done," Jake said bluntly.

"The difficulty," explained Roderick,

is the pitifully short space of time involved. Over a period of months, a great deal might be accomplished. But — in just a fortnight — two weeks . . . ?"

"Two weeks is all we got," growled Jake. "When Mitch climbs outa that coach at the Hortonville depot, we'll be there to meet him — and I want him to see a *new* Kate Jarvis — a genuine, high-falutin' lady."

"Two weeks," Roderick repeated, studying the girl again. "Miss Kate, it seems an impossible task, but, if your father insists . . . "

"Pa's been insistin' — about *everything* — for as long as I can recall," smiled Kate.

"So be it," said Roderick. "I'll do my utmost in the time available." He nodded slowly and traded stares with Jake. "This much I do promise, sir. There'll be a change. Perhaps not a complete transformation, but a change so striking, so dramatic that Mister Mitchel Firestone will be impressed, and I believe this is your aim."

"I don't want for him to notice any other gal but Kate," said Jake.

"Exactly," grinned Roderick. "And so, Mister Jarvis, I accept your proposition. Place your daughter in my hands . . . "

"She's yours — twenty-four hours of the day, if you want," said Jake. "We got a room at Double J you can use, so you'll be right close. No ranch chores for her from now on. She's yours to teach. But no hanky panky, understand? Don't get no fancy ideas of makin' a play for her."

"I have my standards, sir," said Roderick. "Also, I regret to say, a wife who has spurned me. Rest assured I shall conduct myself as a gentleman at all times." He grinned encouragingly at Kate. "Ours will be a teacher-pupil relationship, my dear Miss Kate. You must think of me as your tutor and adviser. As your friend, if you wish, but no more than that."

Some 30 minutes later, while taking

a turn at supervising her roulette layout, Melva Roderick saw her husband shouldering his way through the Coronado's night-time trade and hurrying upstairs to the gallery. Gus Millane, also observing the Englishman's arrival, beckoned a tablehand to take over from him and left his chair at the faro table to come across and talk with his mistress.

"What's he up to now?" he wondered.

"Who knows," she shrugged unconcernedly. "And, if it comes to that, who *cares*?"

"He looked sober — and excited," frowned Millane. A few moments later, glancing to the gallery, he announced, "Here he comes again — toting his valise."

"So he's finally moving out, and that's just fine by me," said Melva.

Roderick carried his bag to the roulette table. The players eyed him impatiently and, after a moment of hesitation, Melva murmured an apology and withdrew a few paces.

"Get it said fast, Roderick," Millane curtly commanded. "You're holding up play."

"There's little to be said anyway," frowned Roderick. "Just — farewell, Melva. I leave tonight, never to return to Omaha."

"Good riddance," she drawled, linking arms with Millane.

The Englishman sighed heavily and turned toward the entrance.

"I've been offered a position," he muttered. "Temporary, but well-suited to my meagre talents. Tried to find the postmaster to advise him of a forwarding address."

"What for?" jeered Millane. "You scarce ever get any mail. "Who'd want to write to a no-account like you?"

"If you'd be so kind, Melva," said Roderick. "One last favor? Not too much to ask, I'm sure. If you'd forward my mail to the Hortonville post office."

"Only one thing I'm sorry for," she murmured. "I'd as soon you were traveling farther than Hortonville."

"No doubt," he said stiffly. "But at least you may be assured I shall never return to Omaha."

He donned his derby and, ignoring the scornful glances of Melva's clients, locals who held all deadbeats in contempt, strode to the entrance and moved out into the night.

At 9 sharp, when the Double J party began the return journey to Horton County, the Englishman shared the wagonseat with Kate. She drove. He talked, quietly, firmly, incessantly, while she hung on his every word. Once, riding within earshot of the rig, Larry heard her repeating, "How nice to see you again, Mitch, and how well you look."

"Remember the lilt," instructed Roderick. "You must learn to vary the tone of your voice by emphasizing certain words, such as 'nice' and 'well'."

"How *nice* to see you again, Mitch," she murmured. "And how *well* you look."

"Better — much better," approved Roderick. "Remembering the rounded vowels. and strive — *strive*, my dear Miss Kate — to abandon the word 'ain't'. Always sound your 'g's'. Never say 'gonna' or gotta'. Remember 'going to' and 'have to' . . . "

The small remuda was moving along steadily, attended by Stretch, Little Jake and the chuck-boss. Rejoining them, Larry rode stirrup-to-stirrup with the runty rancher and eyed him sidelong. Jake returned his glance and growled a warning.

"Don't say it. Don't say *nothin'*. It ain't none of your concern, Valentine."

"He's a panhandler — a bunko-steerer," warned Larry.

"And he ain't even American," muttered Stretch.

"Durn English dude," scowled Curly.

"Which means he's a furriner," declared Stretch.

"You signed on to work cattle, not to butt into my personal affairs!" snapped Jake.

"How much has he taken you for already?" asked Larry.

"Not one bent cent," said Jake. "Two hundred he'll collect — but not till the job's done."

"A job you call it?" challenged Curly. "Him teachin' her all that fancy talk, tryin' to make a lady of her?"

"I call that a lousy insult," protested Stretch. "Any fool could see she's *already* a lady."

"You got a right fine daughter, Jake," Larry pointed out. "How come you ain't satisfied?"

"You think I don't know my own child?" demanded Jake. "Sure she's a lady. But now she has to learn how to *act* and *talk* like a lady! That's what I'm payin' the dude for, savvy?"

"No, he ain't." Jake chuckled harshly. "What the hell's the matter with you, you old hash-slingin' packrat? You think I believe all that hogwash he handed me — 'bout him bein' kin to some English big shot — some barry — barrer . . . ?"

"Barrow-net," offered Curly.

"You think I swallowed that guff?" challenged Jake. "*That'll* be the day! I *know* he's a gyp-artist, just another fancy-talkin' deadbeat. Oh, he's likely a genuine Englisher, but I ain't buyin' that fool story 'bout a castle and servants and meetin' the queen and such."

"And you don't care?" prodded Larry.

"You're finally catchin' on," gibed Jake. "I *don't* care. All I care 'bout is he's educated and needs that two hundred. He's got what I want, and what Kate needs. Enough savvy to school her. By the time he's through with her, she'll be a different gal — different enough to heat Mitch Firestone's blood. Why, I guarantee Kate and Mitch'll be wed inside the half-year."

"Well . . ." Larry shrugged helplessly, "if your mind's made up . . ."

"You better believe my mind's made up, and you better heed what I tell you," growled Jake. "Don't make no trouble for Roderick. Stay clear of him."

He better stay clear of us," countered Stretch. "If I feel his paw in my pocket, I'll bend a gun-barrel over his good-for-nothin' head."

Two hours south of Omaha, they nightcamped in a sheltered grove. Curly built a fire, while the Texans picketed the horses. At Jake's insistence, Kate agreed to bunk inside the wagon, instead of joining the men rolled into their blankets by the fire. The coffeepot chattered and the chuck-boss poured the steaming brew into tin cups. Jake frowned suspiciously, as the Texans prepared to spike their coffee from the whiskey bottle.

"Not for me, old chap," smiled Roderick, watching Curly hold out his cup. "Contrary to what you may have heard in Omaha. I'm not exactly a compulsive toper. I have embarked on an important enterprise, and I shall remain sober and alert until I have properly discharged my responsibilities."

"What he means is he ain't drinkin' no booze," guessed Stretch.

"If that's what he means, why couldn't he say it thataway?"

"He got an education," said Stretch, eyeing the Englishman warily. "One thing I've noticed about educated hombres. They're apt to use more words than they need."

"Touche, Mister Emerson," grinned Roderick. "You're Texan I believe, you and your friend? I find your patois quite fascinating. It has — er — a distinctive quality."

"Thanks for nothin'," growled Stretch.

As Jake held out his cup, Kate adroitly relieved him of it, reached for the coffeepot and asked,

"May I pour for you, Pater?"

"Who — what . . . ?" blinked Jake.

"You didn't notice the difference?" challenged Roderick. "I'm disappointed, Mister Jarvis."

"Well — uh — sure I noticed," frowned Jake. "Only — she never called me *that* before in her whole doggone life!"

Having filled her father's cup, Kate passed it to him.

"I trust it will be to your taste," she smiled.

"Hear that?" Jake challenged the Texans. "She's learnin' already! So *now* how about my wild notion? Not so wild, huh?"

"I ain't surprised," shrugged Larry. "Had Kate pegged for a smart gal the minute I laid eyes on her. A smart gal can learn anything she hankers to learn, I reckon."

"Got me a real fine teacher!" enthused Kate. "It's gonna be a barrel of fun — learnin' how to act like a lady!"

"Caesar's ghost!" groaned Roderick.

"Oh — I am awful sorry . . . " she began.

"Again, if you please," he begged.

"I have a fine teacher," she said carefully. "It is going to be a barrel of . . . "

"I shall enjoy," said Roderick, "would sound so much better."

"I shall enjoy — learning . . . " said Kate.

"To behave as a lady," said Roderick.

" . . . to behave as a lady," finished Kate. She flashed the Texans a wistful smile and confided, "It's what I've always wanted, I guess, only I didn't savvy . . . "

"Didn't realize," corrected Roderick.

"I just didn't realize now much it would mean to me," declared Kate.

"Well said, my dear Miss Kate," nodded the Englishman. "Well said."

★ ★ ★

Next morning, within a quarter-hour of the westbound train dropping a mailsack at the Omaha depot, two letters were delivered to the Coronado Saloon, one addressed to the owner, the other to her husband. Melva Roderick was sharing a late breakfast with Gus Millane, when a barkeep fetched the mail up. After he had left them, she sipped her coffee and glanced at the first letter.

"Anything important?" asked Millane, from his chair by the office window.

"From that same Illinois brewery," she shrugged. "Don't they know we have two breweries right here in Omaha? I should pay freight charges, shipping beer all the way from Lewisburg? No thanks." She tossed that letter aside and glanced at the other, casually at first, then with her eyes dilating. "What — do they *mean*? If this is — somebody's idea of a joke . . . !"

"What's the matter?" demanded Millane.

"Wait till you hear how this letter is addressed," she breathed. "Sir Edward Roderick, Bart, care of Coronado Saloon, Omaha, Nebraska, U.S.A." She frowned perplexedly at him. "What is that supposed to mean? What's a Bart?"

"I think it's short for baronet," said

Millane. "Like you say, sweetheart. Somebody's idea of a joke."

"I'm not so sure." She examined the postmark, turned the envelope over and studied the insignia and scroll. "I've seen this crest before. The couple times Ed got what he called his remittance, it came from this same office. Lawyers in London. And why would they address him as 'Sir'?"

"Good question," drawled Millane. "Go ahead. Read it."

She tore the flap to extract the folded sheet. Millane finished his coffee and lit a cigar, his curious eyes on her flushed face. She was breathing heavily by the time she finished.

"*You* read it!"

He came to the desk, perched on its edge and took the letter from her, and then it was his turn for a violent reaction. His face contorted. An oath erupted from him.

"Read it all," she ordered. "Then tell me what I already know. I shouldn't have let him go!"

Millane read the letter twice.

"All right — I'd say it's plain enough," he muttered. "We figured him for a real Englishman — or maybe a play-actor giving a damn good imitation. And now we know better."

"His father *was* a baronet!" she gasped. "He inherits the title — and everything else!"

"Sir Nigel Roderick has cashed in his chips," frowned Millane, "after making a new will — which means your no-account husband is suddenly rich."

"How rich?" she wondered.

"Figure it out for yourself," scowled Millane. "He gets to be full owner of the family estate, including a castle in Suffolk — with an army of servants. How rich? Richer than you could dream."

"And I never believed him," she fretted. "Every time he talked about it, told how his old man threw him out . . ."

"Why?" interjected Millane.

"Dishonoring the family traditions, the old man said. The way Ed told it, he used to get crazy drunk and gamble his allowance. Seems the old man doted on the elder son, Cedric. And, when Cedric was thrown and killed during a fox hunt . . . "

"That's important — I mean the elder son getting killed. Ed became the old man's next of kin."

"Maybe so, but that's when the old man ran him out of the country. I guess he was mourning Cedric and couldn't stand to have Ed around him."

"But he had a change of heart before he died." Millane nodded thoughtfully. "Made a new will. So, as well as the title, Ed inherits the entire estate."

"Well, damnitall, where does that leave *me*?" demanded Melva. "I took that lily-livered no-account, married him and tried to make something of him. That ought to be worth . . . "

"Take it easy, Melva honey," grinned Millane. "You don't have to settle for a handout. You could have it all."

"You mean . . . ?" she began.

"Think about it." He chuckled elatedly. "You're still his legal wedded wife. You're Ed's next of kin."

"So the law says he has to take care of me — right?" she asked.

"Is that how you want it?" he challenged. "You want to fetch Ed back to Omaha, eat crow, tell him you'll forgive and forget — and then go live with him in England? You relish the idea of being stuck with that fool the rest of your life?"

"It'd be almost worth it," she murmured.

"I got a better idea," he retorted.

"All right." She eyed him expectantly. "I'll listen."

"I said you're his next of kin — you understand what that means?" he asked softly. "It means, sweetheart, if something happens to Ed Roderick — and he ends up dead . . . "

"I get to be a rich widow!" she breathed.

"Everything he had is suddenly

yours," grinned Millane. "You have papers that prove you're the widow of the late Sir Edward Roderick. You take a trip to England and you sell it all, sweetheart, the land, the castle, everything! And you'll be set up for life! No more honky tonks in no more frontier towns."

"You mean for *us*," she smiled. "I'd get lonely, Gus, making that trip to England all by myself."

"I figured to deal myself in," he asured her. "You're gonna need help."

"The kind of help you can arrange," she said quietly. Such as — that fatal accident."

"An accident," he nodded. "Or a bullet. It doesn't much matter, just so long as he ends up dead."

"He'd be in Hortonville by now," she guessed.

"No." He shook his head. "Too soon." He slid from the desk, donned his coat and strode to the door. "More likely he's still on the trail somewhere between here and Horton County.

Won't take me long to find out who hired him, who he's traveling with."

"Do you have to — take care of it personally?" she frowned. "You know all kinds of hard cases, Gus. I'd as soon you let somebody else do it."

"Like you say, I know all kinds," he drawled. "Don't worry, Melva honey. I'll hand this chore to some jasper I can rely on."

It took the gambler less than an hour ro ascertain that Ed Roderick had traveled south from Omaha with a Horton County rancher named Jarvis; a stock-hand at the railroad depot told him all he needed to know. And then, on his way back to the Coronado, Millane sighted the man most likely to fill the role of executioner.

Brett Hawley and his four sidekicks were idling their mounts along the main stem, having just arrived from Hawley's small spread northeast of the big town. He was a hefty, narrow-eyed rogue well known to Millane, an ex-convict of unsavory background. How had Hawley acquired sufficient cash to stock his few acres, after buying the land from old Hub Nixon? Millane figured the answer to that question had been cached somewhere between the territorial prison and the hideout from which Hawley had been taken by a posse. After serving three years of a five-year term, the burly felon was free again and living beyond his means, obviously impatient to get his hands on some big money. At the Coronado, he had gambled heavily and run into debt.

When Millane signaled him from the sidewalk, Hawley shrugged resignedly and muttered a command to his cronies.

"Wait for me at Yerby's. I can guess what Millane's after."

"How much d'you owe the tinhorn anyway?" asked one of his cohorts.

"A thousand," growled Hawley. "And he won't let me forget it."

He turned his mount toward a hitch-rail, while his cronies moved on to Yerby's Bar.

"Let's take a walk," Millane suggested, as Hawley dismounted. "It's time you and me had a little parley."

"I know what's on your mind, Millane," muttered Hawley. "Well, what's your hurry? You offered me time to pay."

"Got a better offer for you," grinned Millane.

They sauntered downtown. He said nothing more until they had reached the loading pens by the railroad and were squatting on a toprail, well out of earshot of passers-by. Hawley accepted a cigar and a light and listened intently, while the gambler explained his proposition in blunt terms. Having said his piece, Millane grinned blandly.

"It's as simple as that, Hawley. You take care of English Eddie. I take care of you. I tear up your I.O.U's. You're no longer in debt to the Coronado."

"Why?" Hawley asked softly. "What's it all about, Millane? What d'you care if that smooth-talkin' deadbeat lives or dies?"

100

"Ask no questions and you'll hear no lies," drawled Millane.

"You'd look damn foolish," warned Hawley, "if I talked to the law — told how you tried to hire me to kill a man."

"You aren't about to do that," chuckled Millane. "I've checked on you. Talkin' to the law — that's not your style."

"I could earn that thousand another way," said Hawley. "Old buddy of mine busted out of the big pen a little while back. I figure to join up with him sometime."

"I don't know if I could persuade my boss to wait that long," said Millane. "Why don't you admit it's an easy chore for you, the easiest way you could get off the hook?"

"Travelin' with old Jake Jarvis, you said," mused Hawley. "I've heard of him. Runs a spread down Horton County way."

"Eddie's with Jarvis, the chuck-boss, Jarvis's daughter and a couple herders," said Millane. "If you move out rightaway, you'll easily overtake 'em before they reach home range. The rest is up to you. Handle it anyway you like, just so long as Eddie Roderick gets his."

"I'd as soon wait to join up with my old buddy, maybe hit a bank or stagecoach," drawled Hawley.

"You can have it both ways," Millane pointed out. "Join up with your friend later. Meanwhile, handle this little chore — and you're out of debt."

"Well, all right then," nodded Hawley. "We'll leave rightaway, likely cut their sign before sundown." He climbed down from the rail and stared up at Millane a moment. "But I'm still curious."

"Never mind about my reasons," said Millane. "Just get it done."

"We'll get it done," Hawley curtly promised. "That cheap panhandler'll never reach Horton County alive."

4

Texts Triggers

MID-AFTERNOON of the second day out of Omaha, the Double J party was overtaken by the five hard cases, but unaware of their proximity. Hawley and his men, after sighting their quarry, veered off the trail and made for the thick grass beyond the brush to the east. The brush shielded them, the grass muffled their horses' hoofbeats, as they pressed on southward, their leader scanning the terrain in search of a safe stakeout.

The wagon, the horsemen and the plodding remuda were a fair distance to their rear, when Hawley spurred his mount to a gallop and made for a rock-littered rise. He growled a command and his cronies tagged him at speed.

"We got time — and plenty of it!" he assured them. "Time to make the top of that hill!"

"Not from *this* side," warned the man moving up level with him. "Too damn steep for the horses!"

"We go around, climb it from the rear," countered Hawley. "And I see a stand of timber less'n a hundred yards east. That's our cover, if we need to make a run for it — which ain't likely."

"If the rear of that rise is as steep as *this* side . . . "

"You worry too much, Peabody. We couldn't be that unlucky."

The east side of the hill proved to be scaleable, for the men if not for their animals. They left the horses ground-hobbled. Hawley and the scrawny Mike Reeve unsheathed their rifles and made for the summit. The others, the pudgy Russ Webb, scar-faced Purdy Barton and the always-fretting Al Peabody clambered after them, their hands on their holsters. Webb and Peabody were panting and sweating by the time they finished the hasty ascent and flopped beside their cohorts.

From the north, the wagon and its escort approached a bend within range of the hill. The chuck-boss was driving, Kate perched beside him, listening attentively to the man riding level with the rig, the man at once recognized by Hawley, who grinned mirthlessly and readied his rifle.

"Easy target, the deadbeat," he remarked to Reeve. "His black jacket shows him clear against the canvas."

"I never much admired English Eddie, him and his smart mouth," muttered Reeve.

"I'll likely score with my first shot," Hawley told the others. "But, in case I miss, you jaspers get ready to hold off the others — keep 'em busy."

"That'll be old Jarvis, other side of the rig," guessed Webbs.

"And his hired hand back there with the remuda," observed Barton.

As his would-be executioner drew a

bead on him, Roderick paid his pupil a compliment.

"I hadn't hoped for such progress in so short a time, Miss Kate. Your speech improves."

"She don't sound like herself, and that's a fact," complained Curly.

"I'm just the same, Curly," Kate good-humoredly assured him. "I sure *feel* the same, but all the better for learnin' — I mean learning — the right way of speaking."

"Miss Kate has a good ear . . . " the Englishman began explaining.

"Two of 'em," grunted the chuck-boss. "And both real purty."

"When I say she has a good ear, I refer to her ability to listen and absorb the mechanics of correct speech," said Roderick.

"Well," shrugged Curly, "long as *you* know what you mean."

"When you're through teaching me, Mister Roderick," said Kate, "maybe you should start on Curly — or Larry or Stretch."

"An impossible task, I'm afraid," grinned Roderick. "Their speech patterns are too firmly established. I fear it is too late for . . ."

He flinched and loosed a startled gasp and, at that same moment, Curly and the girl heard the echo of the rifle-shot. Suddenly Roderick was keeling from his saddle, slumping against the wagon's canopy, his face contorted in pain. The bullet, aimed for the centre of his chest, had come high, creasing his right shoulder and shoving him off-balance. The second bullet, triggered too hastily, plowed through the canopy as he flopped to the dust.

Curly was yelling orders as he jerked back on his reins. Kate back-somersaulted into the wagonbed, while the chuck-boss applied his brake and dropped to the far side of the rig. Coming up from the rear, the Texans bellowed to the cursing Jake to dismount and take cover. The boom of six-shooters was merging with the crackle of riflefire from atop the rise. Fast-triggered slugs kicked up dust, as the drifters swung to the wagon's right side and brought their mounts to a slithering halt.

Watching from along the level barrel of his rifle, Hawley swore bitterly; he had glimpsed his target crawling under the wagon, and realized no mortally-wounded man could move so swiftly.

"You only nicked him," scowled Reeve.

"If I'm lucky, they'll give him a gun and make him lend a hand," muttered Hawley, "and I'll get another shot at him."

"Not so you'd notice," retorted Reeve. "He's no fighter, that no-account dude."

"Keep 'em busy!" Hawley called to the others.

"What the hell d'you think we're *tryin'* to do?" raged Webb.

From behind the stall chuck-wagon, the Texans had opened fire with their Winchesters. Little Jake and Curly were cutting loose with their Colts, but it was the rifle-fire of Larry and Stretch, rapid and too accurate for comfort, that demoralized Webb and Peabody. The Texans aimed at small targets, the barely visible heads and weapons of their attackers, and still wreaked havoc. Webb, lining his Colt on the wagon and trying to draw a bead, heard Reeve's anguished grunt and turned to see the scrawny man leaning forward, both hands clasped to his bloodied face. Hawley made a grab for his stricken crony, but missed. And then, limply, Reeve slid off the summit and down the steep west face of the rise.

A moment later, Peabody glanced to his right and felt his scalp crawl. Purdy Barton had risen to a kneeling position and dropped his pistol. He was gesticulating, but weakly, his eyes dilated in horror, his shirtfront red-streaked from the ugly wound at his throat.

"Oh, hell!" Peabody groaned. "They got Purdy too!"

Barton was trying to rise to his feet when death claimed him. The body fell as Reeve's had fallen, forward and down the steep face of the cliff, to thud to the level ground 50 feet below.

"It's no good, damnitall!" gasped Webb. "We gotta pull out, Brett. We can't get a bead on 'em without showin' ourselves — and two of those jaspers are sharpshooters!"

"I've had enough," mumbled Peabody. "I'm all through." He retreated from the edge, trembling and pallid. "It all went wrong, Brett. If you'd gotten Eddie with your first shot . . . "

"Shuddup, you lousy coward!" snarled Hawley.

"Call *me* coward if you want, but I'm with Al," muttered Webb. He cursed and flinched. A Winchester bullet had whined past his head, almost burning the brim of his Stetson. "The hell with it! I'm quittin' — while I'm still able!"

As Webb and Peabody retreated to the east edge of the summit,

Hawley swore obscenely and levered another slug into his breech. He was determined to take one last shot before hurrying after his badly-scared cronies, but, when he raised himself to seek a target, the Texans quickly discouraged him. They aimed for all they could see of him, his rifle-barrel, the top of his Stetson, and triggered a fast burst, Larry crouched by the tailgate, Stretch hunkered under the vehicle, his Winchester slanted upward with its barrel steadied between the spokes of the left front wheel. Their bullets kicked grit off the edge of the summit inches from Hawley's face. He felt his rifle jerk in his grasp. A slug had struck the barrel. Cursing bitterly, he rolled over and crawled to the east edge of the summit.

By now, Webb and Peabody had descended to the waiting horses and were getting mounted. Hawley called to them angrily, as he came slithering down the slant in a welter of moving dirt and rolling stones.

"Untie those other horses and take 'em along!"

"Listen, all I care about is . . . !" began Peabody.

"Do like I tell you!" raged Hawley. "You want to leave Mike's animal — and Purdy's — so maybe they could be identified?"

Grudgingly, Peabody untethered the riderless horses and began leading them away. Webb followed, hustling his mount to a run. Hawley, the last to move off, sheathed his rifle and glared back at the rise. Somewhere beyond, shielded by the wagon, were his intended victim and the gun-smart strangers who had proved more than a match for Reeve and Barton.

"They're gonna pay for this," he vowed, as he sank spur and started his mount galloping toward the timber. "But — first — I'll get some answers from that smart-talkin' tinhorn. He owes me, damn him! he owes me!"

The taller Texan, warily scanning

the summit of the rise, called to his partner.

"Runt, what d'you think?"

"Everybody stay low," Larry called to the others. Then, dropping his voice, he told Stretch, "I think they've quit, but let's make damn sure."

They held their positions, Kate lying face-down amid the clutter of provisions and cooking gear in the wagonbed, Jake and Curly hunkered beside the wounded Englishman on the other side of the rig, the Texans readying their rifles and watching the summit.

"Damn-blasted sidewinders . . . !"

Jake began a booming tirade, but was curtly silenced by Larry.

"Save your bull-roarin', Jake! We're tryin' to hear!"

"Who's the boss and who's the hired hand?" gasped Jake. "You mind how you talk to me, Valentine." He hesitated a moment, then asked, "Tryin' to hear *what*?"

"That," growled Larry.

They all heard it then, far-off but

distinct, the steady thud of hooves.

"Could be a trick," Stretch warned. "They send one man away with the horses to make us think they've quit — while the others wait up top there . . . "

"Ready to gun the first one shows his head, huh?" prodded Curly.

"Kate . . . ?" began Jake.

"I ain't hurt, Pa!" she called. "Damn canvas is riddled, but they didn't score on me!"

"Miss Kate — *please*!" groaned Roderick.

After a brief pause, the blonde girl rephrased her announcement.

"I am not hurt, Pater."

Larry retreated from the tailgate, moving around to remount. He slid his rifle into its scabbard and called to his partner.

"You know what to do."

"Yup," grunted Stretch. "When you make your break, I'll give you coverin' fire — if I have to."

"I say, Valentine, old chap . . . !"

Roderick rolled over and gaped incredulously at the mounted Texan. "Surely you don't mean to — deliberately expose yourself . . . ?"

"They won't see all that much of me," muttered Larry.

He resorted to an old Indian trick as he raced his mount away from the wagon, swinging from his saddle and clinging to the animal's left side. Had the attackers stayed atop the rise, they would have sighted only the moving pony and maybe a glimpse of Larry's right boot atop its rump and part of his right arm braced on its shoulders. In that way, he traveled around the rise to its east side, reaching it in time to see three riders disappearing into the timber, the third man leading two riderless horses.

Raising himself into his saddle, he walked his pony around to the other side, pausing at the base of the steeper slant to study the crumpled bodies of Mike Reeve and Purdy Barton. He called to his companions and they broke cover. Kate clambered from the wagon, ordering Curly to remove the Englishman's upper garments, demanding that her father hunt up firewood.

"Got to doctor him rightaway," she pointed out. "Who's gonna be my teacher, if Mister Roderick takes blood poisoning?"

"Curly, fetch Roderick over here," commanded Larry. "Kate, you stay where you are."

Stretch crawled from under the rig, sheathed his rifle and helped get the Englishman upright.

"It's not — so terribly painful," mumbled Roderick. "A flesh-wound, I presume."

"I'll tote you," offered Stretch.

"No need," Roderick assured him. "No need."

They moved across to stand beside Larry, who had rolled the dead men over and was studying their contorted faces, while going through their pockets.

"How about it?" he demanded.

"Anybody ever see these hombres before? How about you, Roderick?"

Roderick clenched his teeth and fought against his nausea; in death, the faces of the Texans' victims were no pleasant sight.

"Don't waste no sympathy on 'em," drawled Stretch. "This wasn't no tea-party, mister."

"It was an ambush," the chuck-boss said flatly. "And I don't savvy what they were after. Why ambush a chuck-wagon? Did they need supplies so bad — or were they after our horses?"

"They creased Roderick with their first shot," said Larry. "Seems to be *he's* the one they wanted. And I mean dead."

"But that's ridiculous — most outlandish idea I've ever heard," protested Roderick. He grimaced uncomfortably. "The simple fact is — I'm of no real importance — to anybody."

"Look at those faces again," ordered Larry. "You know 'em?"

"They're-vaguely familiar," frowned

117

Roderick. "But I can't name them. I suppose I've seen them — somewhere in Omaha. Ranch-workers, I think."

"What'd you find?" Curly asked Larry.

"Nothin' to identify 'em," said Larry. "Less'n a dollar in small change. The usual stuff a ranch-hand'd have in his pockets. Nothin' with a name on it." He nodded to the Englishman. "You get on back to the wagon. I guess Kate knows how to patch a gunshot wound."

"What will you do . . . ?" Roderick gestured nervously to the dead men. "About them, I mean. Should we take them with us, deliver them to the Horton County undertaker? You can't just — leave them here — surely . . . "

"Burial detail," shrugged Stretch.

"Pardon?" asked Roderick.

"We'll plant 'em," Larry said gruffly. "What else?"

"Ain't the first time we had to fight off bushwackers," Stretch calmly assured the Englishmen. "We've done it before — and we'll likely have to do it again."

Later, squatting in the shade of the stalled wagon, stripped to the waist and submitting to Kate's rough but effective doctoring, Roderick stared soberly at Jake Jarvis and declared,

"I'll never get used to it — the violence of this harsh land." His gaze drifted to the craggy ridges away to the west, a butte on the horizon, its ugly bulk soaring to the sky, and the yucca-dotted prairie sprawling away from the trail. "I find myself — yearning for familiar scenes, the soft beauty of Suffolk with its rolling downs, the colors so muted, the life so gentle — compared with here. And the people . . . " he winced to the sound of spades digging into hard ground; over by the base of the rise, the Texans were preparing to bury the dead ambushers. "Valentine and his friend. Callous — in such a casual, off-hand way. They don't react as civilized human beings."

"If they wasn't so gun-smart, if they didn't move so damn fast and slick," growled Jake, "might've been more'n one of us wounded. Might be some of us dead — maybe *all* of us." He grimaced impatiently, nudged a Long 9 into his mouth and scratched a match for it. "They got too much sass for my likin'. But, in this kinda ruckus, I'd as soon have'em fightin' for me than against me."

"I'm sorry if this hurts, Mister Roderick," said Kate.

"How bad was he hit?" demanded Jake.

"Right shoulder creased," she told him. "I don't reckon the slug hit bone . . . "

"Flesh wound," grunted Roderick.

"Even so, when we get home, we ought to have Doc Dudley check him over," she opined. She finished binding the wound. Roderick mumbled his thanks and reached for his clothes. "You take it easy from here on, Mister Roderick."

"He don't need to ride no more," decided Jake. "Better if he travels in the rig."

"No need to treat me as an invalid," frowned Roderick.

"I got an investment in you, mister," Jake reminded him. "We made a deal, and I'm holdin' you to it, so you gotta stay healthy enough to finish your chore."

Curly and the Texans returned. There was little to show for their efforts, just a couple of barely discernible mounds over by the base of the rise, and Roderick was shocked by their attitude. They had fought off an ambush, killing two of their attackers in the process. And now, less than 30 minutes later, they were nonchalantly rolling cigarettes, making ready to move on. Curly was a mite preoccupied, but Kate and her cantankerous sire seemed just as philosophical as the Texans.

"Still think they were out to kill the dude?" Curly challenged.

"Aimed their first shot at him, didn't they?" shrugged Larry.

"My hunch is they planned on hijacking the rig and horses," growled Jake. "Only reason Roderick stopped the first bullet, he was likely the clearest target. Why would anybody want to kill a deadbeat anyway?" he thought to assure the haggard Englishman, "No offense, but you gotta admit I'm makin' sense. Why *would* anybody . . . ?"

"Why indeed?" sighed Roderick. "I consider myself worthless — dead or alive."

Larry lit his cigarette and squinted to the south, remarking,

"I'm tryin' to recall how close we are."

"We'll make the old line-shack on Moose Ridge by sundown — maybe an hour after," said Jake. "Better we nightcamp there. Easier on Roderick. We push on after sun-up and, by noon, we'll see Double J range." As he remounted, he frowned at Larry and asked, "You thinkin' they'll try us again?"

"Quien sabe?" shrugged Larry.

The shack on the bald ridge proved to be a weather-battered structure with a sagging roof, rickety furniture, a usable stove and sleeping accommodation for three line-riders. Kate insisted she would again sleep in the wagon, so that her father, tutor and the chuck-boss could use the bunks. Though he thought it unlikely the ambushers were trailing them, Larry was disinclined to take chances. A fire would burn out front of the shack throughout the night, and the drifters would take turns to patrol the ridge.

An hour after supper, while they hunkered by the fire, about to flip a dime to decide who should take first turn at guard duty, the Englishman emerged from the shack and moved across to join them. Jake and the chuck-boss had fallen asleep. Kate had retired to the wagon.

"A trifle stuffy in there," muttered

Roderick. He squatted beside Stretch, a blanket draped about his shoulders. "Mind if I join you a while?"

"Help yourself," drawled the taller Texan. "We ain't all that particular."

"The same note of scepticism." Roderick heaved a sigh and frowned reproachfully at them. "In Omaha, I thought I'd become hardened to it. I was reduced to the indignity of trying to borrow money from the honest burghers of that town . . ."

"On account of you're too blame lazy to work for your livin'," Larry sourly accused.

"I wish I could make you understand," muttered Roderick. "You see, it's all true. I've never lied about myself. I am Edward Giles Roderick, second son of Sir Nigel Roderick of Suffolk . . ."

"Oh, sure," grinned Stretch.

"The blood of true British nobility flows in my veins," Roderick doggedly assured them.

"He bled some when that bullet nicked him," Stretch reminded Larry.

"So what he says is *part* true. He's got blood."

"Try to understand my position," begged Roderick. "I didn't really mind, when the citizens of Omaha scoffed at me. I suppose, as I said before, I became hardened to it. But, with you gentlemen, it's different. Suddenly it's important to me — terribly important — that I convince you I am what I claim to be."

"A rich dude," jeered Stretch.

"*I'm* not wealthy," frowned Roderick. "But my father . . ."

"He's got all the dinero," drawled Larry. "Only he don't much care about you, so he sent you all the way to America — just to be rid of you?"

"That's the truth!" Roderick said earnestly. "How — how did you guess?"

"Aw, for Pete's sake . . ." Stretch grimaced in exasperation.

"You gotta admit he thinks fast," grinned Larry. "That brain of his never stops workin'."

"But that's exactly the way it happened," declared Roderick. "My father — expelled me from the family home." He shrugged sadly. "Not that I blame him. Poor old warrior. He was grief-stricken, when my brother was killed. Cedric was the elder son, you see. The old man had such high hopes for him. Stout fellow, Cedric. Expert horseman, fine all-round sportsman and brilliant student, when we were at Cambridge. Ideal type for carrying on the family tradition, you know. As for me — well — I was the ne'er-do-well — a loafing parasite . . . "

"What d'you mean 'was'?" challenged Larry.

"Terrible shock for the old man — Cedric's death," muttered Roderick, staring moodily into the fire. "Mother had died some ten years before. I was a poor substitute for Cedric — a thorn in his side — a constant disappointment. And, suddenly, he couldn't bear the sight of me. He paid my passage to this

126

country, ordered me never to return to England and arranged to contribute to my support. But, of course, this was a mere pittance, barely enough to keep body and soul together. And that's why I was — obliged to become little better than a beggar."

"I'm gonna bust out cryin' any minute now," announced Stretch, yawning boredly.

"I hoped for some improvement of my social and financial situation, when I married Melva," said Roderick. "She owns a saloon in Omaha, the Coronado, quite a profitable concern. I was devoted to her, I assure you, but it seems I overestimated her regard for me." He shrugged resignedly. "It's not the sort of thing a man wants to admit, but I suppose I have to face up to it. Melva never really cared for me. I had a certain — novelty value — I suppose."

"She threw you out — and who could blame her?" growled Larry. "Save your breath, deadbeat. You're some helluva liar, but you'll never convince us, never in a million years."

"What's the matter, Ed?" grinned Stretch. "You think you're the first panhandler we ever run into — think we never met your kind before?"

"It's all true!" protested Roderick.

"Oh, sure," chuckled Stretch.

"If your old man's a big shot — with a castle and all . . . " began Larry.

"A baronet — a landowner," Roderick assured him.

"Sam Houston."

"And I'm Davy Crockett," drawled Stretch.

"You — don't believe me," sighed Roderick.

"What you need, Ed, is a new pitch," advised Stretch.

"A different story," nodded Larry. "Somethin' folks're apt to buy." He jerked a thumb. "Better take care of that wound. Get on back to your bunk and catch your sleep. This Nebraska weather is murder on deadbeats."

"I have failed — in more ways than

one," Roderick lamented, as he rose to his feet. "I'm an unsuccessful liar, but even less convincing when I tell the truth."

He returned to the shack. Stretch flipped a dime and won the privilege of sleeping by the fire till midnight, while Larry prowled back and forth along the top of the ridge, probing the moonlit terrain surrounding them, his ears alert for the sound of hoofbeats. In the hour after midnight, he moved down to the fire, tossed more wood onto it and roused his partner. Stretch patrolled until the daybreak, when Kate climbed from the wagon to help Curly fix breakfast; the night had passed without incident.

Roderick and the Texans broke out their shaving gear. While they plied their razors, Little Jake trudged back and forth, fidgetting, reminding them of the chores in store for them upon their arrival at the Double J. He was short-tempered before the first meal of the day — and at all other times.

"Turnin' Kate over to you," he told the Englishman. "Only time you let up is when you stop to eat. From sun-up to when she hits the feathers, you'll be schoolin' her, savvy?"

"That's understood, sir," nodded Roderick. "Be assured I shall do my best for her."

"As for you two smart-alecks . . . " began Jake.

"Ranch chores," drawled Larry, as his keen blade moved down his left cheek. "That's what we signed on for."

"We're yours for the whole month, Jake," said Stretch. "You don't need to fret about us. We can handle any chores you got. Horses that need breakin', cattle to be branded, fences to be fixed. You name it. We can handle it."

"Soon as we eat, we move on," announced Jake. "Oughta be home by noon." He turned to glower at the chuck-boss. "What's holdin' up that chow?"

"Come and get it," shrugged Curly. "It's been ready this past five minutes. Couldn't tell you on accounta you was runnin' off at the mouth — just like always."

* * *

Mid-morning of that day, Brett Hawley and his surviving cohorts returned to Omaha. The ex-convict had set a stiff pace in his eagerness to confront and challenge Gus Millane and, by the time they reached the big town's southern outskirts, their animals were lathered and panting.

Webb's clothes clung tight to his flabby frame, damp with sweat. He was sullen and silent, blaming Hawley for their reversal, but intimidated by Hawley's fury and keeping his thoughts to himself. Not so the shattered Peabody. He talked incessantly.

"I was never that close before," he mumbled, as they made for a side alley. "Never that close to — a couple jaspers

131

that got it. I ain't never gonna forget how Purdy looked — and Mike too — just before they fell down that slant. Oh, hell! All that blood on Mike's face . . . !"

"Will you *shuddup*?" snarled Hawley.

"You don't care, Brett," chided Peabody. "I swear you don't care a damn about Mike and Purdy. And why'd we ride with you anyway? What was in it for us? You said let's go, and we went along — and now Mike and Purdy are done for."

"No wonder that ambush blew up in our faces," scowled Hawley. "If I'd had goodmen backin' me — instead of a bunch of yeller-bellied no-accounts . . . !"

"Them herders was real sharpshooters," complained Peabody.

"Why couldn't I find Corbett and his pards? That's a rough outfit — smart hombres that don't lose their nerve when the chips're down" Hawley swore bitterly. "I'd do better with Corbett than with the likes of you."

132

"No use you bullyin' Millane — if that's what you're plannin'," offered Webb. "You're still into him for a thousand."

"What I got to say to Millane is none of your damn business," countered Hawley.

In the alley beside the Coronado, they dismounted. Hawley surrendered his rein to Webb and growled orders.

"Take our animals to Harkin's barn."

"And how do we pay for their feed?" demanded Webb.

"Tell Harkin to send a bill to the Coronado," muttered Hawley.

"I need a drink — awful bad," sighed Peabody.

"Drink all you want at the Coronado," said Hawley, grinning mirthlessly. "I reckon Millane owes us that much."

While Webb walked the horses to the Harkin livery stable, Hawley barged into the barroom of the Coronado with Peabody at his heels. A barkeep greeted them with a curt nod and, in answer to Hawley's question, jerked a thumb toward the stairs.

"Up in the boss's office," he drawled. Winking, grinning knowingly, he added, "They're together all the time, now that Eddie's quit."

"We're Millane's guests, understand?" said Hawley. "You take care of Peabody and Webb." As he turned away, he told the trembling hard case, "Drink all you want — and maybe you'll get your nerve back."

"I'll never feel the same," mumbled Peabody.

A few moments after Hawley had climbed the stairs, Webb came trudging in. He joined Peabody at the bar, accepted the drink poured for him by the barkeep and swigged greedily.

"Upstairs with Millane, is he?" he asked.

"Yeah, sure," grunted Peabody. "And what I want to know is how can that help Mike and Purdy — him cussin' that tinhorn?"

"Well, I ain't much interested," lied

Webb. He finished his drink and turned away. "Think I saw a feller I used to know, when I came out of Harkin's. Guess I'll go talk to him while we're waitin' for Brett. I'll be back in a little while."

After quitting the barroom, the flabby malcontent retreated into the side alley and made for the firestairs leading up to the balcony of Melva Roderick's private quarters. More than curious, he had become suspicious of Hawley, regarding him as directly responsible for the deaths of Reeve and Barton. Had Hawley expressed some small regret, he might have felt differently. But the ex-convict had seemed more impatient than saddened by the violent demise of two loyal followers. Why had Hawley insisted on challenging Millane in private, out of earshot of his cronies? To get answers, Russ Webb was willing to eavesdrop. Noting that the window was half-open, he darted a glance along the valley. Then, satisfied that his movements were unobserved, he quietly climbed the firestairs. He was squatting close by the window, listening intently, when Melva Roderick gasped an anguished protest.

"Don't hit him again — *please* . . . !"

Millane was half-sprawled across the desk. The dark-haired beauty had retreated to a corner, her hands clasped to her breasts, her eyes wide with fright. Panting heavily, raising a hand to his bloodied mouth, the gambler slid from the desk and tried to stay on his feet. Hawley seized him by his shirtfront, shoved him into a chair and stood over him, his fists clenched.

"I'll say it just one more time," he breathed. "Unless this lousy tinhorn talks, I'll fix him so his own mother wouldn't recognize him." He grinned coldly at the woman. "You got any notion what a fist could do — to that handsome face of his? You ready to see it, lady?"

"Don't . . . !" she began.

"By the time I'm through with him, you couldn't stand to look at him," warned Hawley. "You'd be sick to your stomach."

"He's — out of his mind . . . " groaned Millane.

"The hell I'm out of my mind," gibed Hawlkey. "I'm smart enough to know you had a reason, Millane, and I'm bettin' it's important. Somethin' big. What d'you care if English Eddie lives or dies? He'd left Omaha anyway. And even if he'd stayed, he's too weak to make trouble for you and his woman."

"None of your business, Hawley!" gasped Millane.

"I lost two men when I ambushed Jarvis's party," Hawley retorted. "And it might've been worse — and that *makes* it my business!" He grasped Millane's cravat, jerked him half-upright and drew back his bunched right. "Why'd you want him killed? You're gonna tell me — here and now — or I'll work on your face till . . . !"

"Please . . . !" cried Melva.

"No use beggin'," warned Hawley.

"Only one way you can save him. I asked a question, and I want an answer — *now*!"

"We were — all wrong about Ed." She sighed heavily, advanced from the corner and sank into her chair. "A letter came for him. He really is — the son of a rich Englishman — a baronet. And his father died a few weeks back."

"Meanin' Roderick inherits?" challenged Hawley. He released Millane, who slumped low in his chair. "Well, well, well! Now ain't *that* somethin'! How much?"

"I don't know," she frowned.

"Don't play games with me," he growled.

"All right, all right." She shrugged helplessly. "The whole fortune left by his father. Ed's next in line to inherit, under the terms of the old man's will."

"So, if Roderick dies, *you* inherit!" Hawley bared his teeth in a grin, swaggered across to the liquor cabinet and poured himself a drink. "*That's* why he has to go. Why, sure! You collect and, as soon as all that cash is in your greedy hands, you and the tinhorn hitch up and live easy the rest of your lives."

"You had to tell him" scowled Millane.

"He'd have marked you for life," she murmured. "I couldn't let him do that, Gus. Not to you."

"Nothin's changed," chuckled Hawley. He took a stiff pull at the raw bourbon and smacked his lips. "You'll get what you want, Melva. Well — *most* of it." He studied them triumphantly, enjoying their dismay. "Yeah, you guessed it. I'm dealin' myself in — for a third."

"Damn you, Hawley . . . !" began Millane.

"What's to argue about?" shrugged Hawley. "Gonna be plenty for all of us."

"You and your hard case sidekicks," sneered Millane.

"Hell, no," grinned Hawley. "I got no use for Peabody or Webb — that lard-bellied no-account. It's gonna be our secret, Millane. Just me and you and Melva." He snapped his fingers. "You go buy us a couple good horses. We'll be leavin' for Horton County in a little while."

"Hold on now . . . " began Millane.

"I'll take care of Roderick, but I want you along," Hawley declared. "I don't trust you, tinhorn. I want you where I can see you." Eyeing the woman defiantly, he warned her, "He's my insurance. I figure you'll keep your beautiful mouth shut, hold to your end of our bargain, if I keep the tinhorn with me."

"A third he says," muttered the gambler.

"And, when it's all over, no chance of a double-cross, drawled Hawley. "You try turnin' me in, and *you're* gallows-bait — you and your woman. The law would call you equal guilty. That much I know for a fact."

"We have no choice," said Melva.

"No choice," Millane sourly agreed.

"Not the way he deals the cards."

"Between here and Horton, if you got any idea of jumpin' me, forget it," advised Hawley. "I sleep with one eye open." He gestured impatiently. "Go on. Go buy those horses."

Webb had beaten a hasty retreat. He was at the bar again, drinking with Al Peabody, when Hawley descended from the gallery.

5

Gilding of the Lily

HAWLEY'S instructions were delivered curtly. He ordered his cohorts to return to the ranch and await him there. Unfinished business required his attention.

"Just keep an eye on the stock and take it easy. I'll be back in a week — maybe sooner."

"More likely never," Webb was thinking, as he watched the hefty schemer walk out. "You'd let us stay on. You wouldn't care if we starved. And, while we starved, you'd be countin' your share of the Roderick fortune. Well, damn you, Brett Hawley, I got a better idea."

Later, riding slowly northeast of Omaha, leading the animals once ridden by Reeve and Barton, the pudgy man and the dispirited Peabody discussed their uncertain future. Webb wasn't about to confide the important information he had overheard, eavesdropping outside Melva Roderick's window. He confined his comments to a few remarks about the abortive ambush, an incident Peabody was anxious to forget.

"What I mean is I hope I can forget," mumbled Peabody. "Hell, Russ, that sound Purdy made — it wasn't human!"

"You keep gabbin' about it and you'll *never* forget," warned Webb.

"I tell you, Russ, I've had my bellyful," confided Peabody. "It's enough to make a man go straight. What kind of a future would I have — followin' a jasper as mean as Brett?" He fished out a kerchief, mopped at his brow and stared thoughtfully to the northern horizon. "I got a mind to quit, while I still got my health."

"Well," shrugged Webb, "Hawley ain't here to stop you. No tellin' when he'll get back."

"You gonna quit too?"

"Guess so, Al."

"Tag along with me then! I carve to try my luck up Dakota way."

"Not for me, Al. There's a warrant out for me in Dakota. West'd be a sight healthier for me. I'll make for the Wyomin' Territory."

"So, uh, we just pack what grub we can find at the spread and get the hell outa Nebraska?"

"That's for me."

"Well, okay then. That'll suit me fine."

By noon, the survivors of Brett Hawley's unsavory quartet had gone their separate ways, Peabody pushing north to follow the Elkhorn River route, Webb riding a wide half-circle around Omaha and swinging to the south, all the time alert for a glimpse of two other riders — Hawley and Millane. The pudgy hard case had made his decision. He lacked the courage to openly defy Hawley, to accuse him of disloyalty to his men. But he had devised another and safer means of punishing his one-time leader. If he could reach Horton ahead of Hawley and the gambler, get to the Englishman and warn him, there would be no fortune for the treacherous trio. And Roderick would be only too eager to pay for this warning. How much was his life worth to him? This was the question Webb would ask.

About to hustle his mount over the bald summit of a hill, he changed his mind, reined up and dismounted. Then, climbing to the summit on hands and knees, he dropped flat and surveyed the land to the northeast.

"Already I'm outsmartin' you — you double-crossin' buzzard. If I'd ridden up here, you'd have spotted me for sure."

The distance was considerable, but he recognized the two horsemen following the stage-route. Calculating he had a two hour start on them he returned to his horse and swung astride. For the next five miles he traveled patches of thick brush, the timbered hogsbacks and the beds of dried-out arroyos, giving the regular trail a wide berth. The would-be assassins weren't hustling. So much the better for him. "You'll find him Brett," he reflected. "But not before I do!"

★ ★ ★

At about the same time that Russ Webb was checking the stage-route from his lofty vantage point, Little Jake's party was arriving at the Double J headquarters. The three hired hands emerged to greet them, tagged by their families and, for a few moments, the runty rancher was hard-pressed to get a word in edgewise. Kate made quite a ceremony of introducing her tutor, who bemused the ranch-hands by doffing his derby and bowing low to their gingham-gowned womenfolk. Larry and Stretch traded good-humored greetings with the children, while off-saddling the horses and turning the remuda into a corral, and Curly Becker unloaded the rig and tended his team.

"That's enough jawin'!" Jake bellowed. "C'mon now, we all got chores! Get back to work all of you! Kate, you take your teacher-man into the house, get him settled into that spare room. Valentine, Emerson, switch your saddles to fresh horses and go scout the chaparral. That's where Double J bunch-quitters always stray — consarn their hides. Deke! What the hell am I payin' you for? Supposed to be my ramrod, ain't you? Go on! Saddle up and show 'em the way — else they're apt to get lost!" He grinned coldly at the Texans. "Maybe find 'emselves flushin' Hammerhead strays."

"Keep your shirt on, old timer," grinned Stretch. "We can tell one brand from another."

"Don't call me old!" chided Jake. "I ain't so old I couldn't whup the tar outa you!"

"Forgettin' somethin', ain't you, Jake?" The ramrod, Deke Finlay, was a lean and weathered veteran, too long a Double J hand to be intimidated by his boss's bombast. "I make it eatin' time. First we eat. Then I'll take Larry and Stretch out to the chaparral."

"We ain't had lunch!" Jake suddenly realized.

"When a man starts forgettin' such things . . ." Finlay aimed a wink at the Texans, "that's a sure sign he's past his prime — gettin' too old to . . ."

"Don't *you* start on me!" warned Jake. "Don't push your luck, Deke! I'm some shorter'n you, but I ain't puny. I could whup you . . ."

"With one had tied behind your back," nodded the ramrod.

"Everybody eat!" ordered Jake. "Then get on with the chores!"

By 2 p.m., the Texans were scouting the timbered sections of Double J range, flushing out the strays and running them back to grazeland. To a couple of nomads raised in cattle country, these routine tasks were like therapy;

they worked automatically, with the practised skill of veteran cattlemen, and were mentally relaxed, able to forget yesterday's bloodshed, the ambush and its grim aftermath.

In the parlor of the Jarvis home, his strength boosted by a substantial meal, Roderick put his pupil through her paces.

"A lady never trudges never slouches." He followed her actions intently, as she moved about the room, responding to his directions. "A lady moves gracefully at all times, the back always straight, the head held high, the shoulders never slumped. That's better. Ah, yes. Excellent. Now take a seat — and remember — you *lower* yourself into the chair. You never flop."

"This way?" she asked, seating herself slowly.

"Better all the time," he nodded. "And the hands, my dear. Never give the impression you don't know what to do with your hands. When in doubt, simply clasp them in your lap. That's right. And now you may offer me a drink."

"You thirsty already?" she frowned.

"This is make-believe," he explained. "I want you to go through the motions of serving refreshments. *Pretend* to wait on me — you understand?"

"I guess so." She nodded eagerly, rose from her chair and retreated to a corner. "All right then. I'll pretend this is a table with a lot of booze and glasses and . . . "

"Liquor," correct Roderick. He shuddered in horror. "Booze! Miss Kate, have mercy, I beg you. Never use that word again."

"Whatever you say," she shrugged. "All right. You ready?"

"Ready," said Roderick.

"How should I ask you?" she demanded.

"Just ask," he urged. "I'll be ready to correct you."

She smiled invitingly.

"All right, Mister Roderick, what'll you have?" He sighed heavily and shook

150

his head. "Well — uh — name your poison, mister." He covered his face with his hands. "Well, heck, Mister Roderick, that's what Pa always says, when he's invitin' — I mean inviting some feller to drink with him."

"I have no doubt," muttered Roderick.

"How about — uh — name your pleasure?" she asked.

"Almost acceptable, but not quite," said Roderick. "Now try this. May I offer you some refreshment, Mister Roderick?"

"May I offer you some refreshment, Mister Roderick?"

"Much better." He smiled approvingly. "And now your guest responds. By your leave madam, perhaps a little whiskey — and so forth. And another thing. A gentleman always requests permission before smoking. A dignified nod is sufficient in such cases. Or, alternatively, if you anticipate his need for a cigar, you may gesture — like so — and say 'Smoke, if you wish.'"

"Like this . . . ?"

"Very Good, Miss Kate. We progress."

"What next? More walking?"

"By all means. A circuit of the room, if you please. Imagine you're strolling the boardwalk of the main street, being greeted by friends and acquaintances. And remember the response must be dignified — friendly — but dignified. Proceed."

Kate began an unhurried circuit of the room, and the Englishman was profoundly impressed. His task was being made easier by the girl's adaptability; he hadn't dared hope she would respond so readily to his instructions. The shirt and blue jeans, though unconventional, emphasized her neat figure and the all-important fact that she was learning to move gracefully; the girl was fast acquiring poise.

"You pause to exchange greetings," he ordered. "An elderly lady accompanied by a small child. Go ahead. Improvise."

"Good morning, Mrs Kelso." She nodded politely. "And how is your husband this fine day?"

"The child," prodded Roderick.

"And little Melissa," smiled Kate. "Looking prettier than ever. How's that?"

"No criticism," frowned Roderick. "Continue." She resumed her stroll. "You respond to another greeting. This time let's suppose a passing rider, a ranch-hand, calls to you . . ."

"And they all do," she cheerfully assured him. "Every cowpoke in the territory."

"Yes, I assume you're a most popular young lady," said Roderick. "I also assume the ranch-hand would greet you as he might greet any woman of the town — including those employed in the saloons. We have to draw a line of distinction here — do you understand? He calls to you. Probably he waves to you.

"I — don't wave back?" she frowned.

"You're learning." he smiled triumphantly. "My compliments, Miss Kate. Obviously there are many points that need not be stressed. You're developing

153

the instincts, as well as the actions, of a true lady. So how do you respond to the greeting of a passing rider?"

"Just a nod," she guessed.

"Excellent," said Roderick. "And now you move on."

"A few minutes later, Little Jake came to the parlor doorway and squinted at his slow-pacing daughter.

"Where you headed?" he demanded.

"Nowhere," she replied, still walking. Jake frowned perplexedly at the Englishman and asked,

"If she ain't headed noplace, how come she keeps movin'?"

"Your daughter is practising her walk," Roderick explained.

"What kinda foolery is this?" Jake challenged. "She learned to walk when she was so high. How come she gotta practise?"

"Now, Pater, you promised to let Mister Roderick teach me the right way of everything," Kate reminded him. "And that includes walking — the way a lady should walk."

"Gotta admit I never seen her walk thataway before," mused Jake. "Moves along real easy, huh Roderick? Like a thoroughbred filly."

"One of those vital details, sir," drawled the Englishman. "The favorable impression of correct speech could be discounted by awkward movements. For example, a clumsy, plodding walk."

"I don't savvy half of what he says," Jake remarked to his daughter, "but I guess it makes sense." He scratched at his stubbly jowls and grinned approvingly. "Mister, I don't care what kind of deadbeat you've been, just so long as you can teach her what she needs to know. And I reckon you're doin' it. Yes siree, boy, you're gettin' results."

"You notice an improvement?" asked Roderick.

"I sure do." As he retreated, Jake eyed his mobile offspring again and voiced an afterthought. "All I hope is, when she meets young Mitch again, she won't be wore out from all this traipsin' — too weary to stand up and tell him howdy."

"When young Mister Firestone returns to Hortonville, he'll be greeted by a lady of poise and assurance," Roderick promised. After the little man had left them, he gestured for his pupil to take a break. "Rest yourself, Miss Kate. Could we now discuss another important aspect of your grooming? Your wardrobe, my dear."

"You mean new duds?" she asked, resuming her chair.

"Pardon?" He frowned severely. "I presume you meant to say new clothes?"

"Oops," said Kate. "All right, what about clothes? I never worried much about prettying up. Got just two gowns, one for going to church. One for dancing at the church socials."

"I recommend the purchase of a new gown, several new gowns in fact," said Roderick. "With, of course, matching accessories. You'll need hats — fashionable, but not too garish."

"I wouldn't know how to . . . "

"Don't worry. I'll choose everything."

"You mean — *everything*?"

Only your outer garments, naturally.

"Oh. I guess you mean — uh — we'll let Lulu decide what I ought to wear underneath."

After a moment of hesitation, Roderick enquired,

"Who, may one ask, is Lulu?"

"Lulu Duprez," said Kate. "She runs the best ladies store in Hortonville. All the rich women, like Mayor Kelso's wife and Mrs Firestone and Amy Carew that owns the Lucky Deck Casino . . . "

"Mrs Carew — *who* owns the casino," corrected Roderick.

"She's not married." Kate giggled behind her hand and blushed a little. "But a lot of folks claim she *ought* to be."

"To return to Miss Duprez," frowned Roderick. "I'll assume she can supply a suitable selection. If, as you say, her establishment is patronized by the local ladies of quality."

"That's right. Only the best folks buy

from Lulu, on account of her stuff costs more."

"The afternoon is young," remarked Roderick, glancing at the clock. "Perhaps, if your father would send for her, Miss Duprez might consent to make the journey from the township, fetching a selection of her finest merchandise."

"You want Lulu to bring my new clothes out here?" frowned Kate.

"Would that be too much to ask?"

"Heck, no! Lulu would travel ten miles — on her hands and knees — to sell a spool of thread at her own price. She's some businessman, that Lulu."

"You mean businesswoman. French, of course."

"No. And it's not Miss. It's Mrs. She's a widow. Her husband was a New Orleans man."

"Well then, my dear, shall we send for her?"

Within the quarter-hour, Deke Finlay's eldest son was headed for town on a fast-running pony, bound for Madame

Lulu's Bon Ton to deliver a note written hastily by Little Jake himself.

The overweight widow, after reading the note, gleefully announced to her assistant,

"That sawn-off old hothead finally came to his senses! Seems he's ready to admit Kate's his daughter, and not a son. And not before time, by golly!"

For the benefit of her well-heeled clients, Lulu Duprez affected the genteel speech of a lady of fashion. With only her assistant to hear, she reverted to the rough language of her early days; she was twice a widow, her first husband having been a roughneck mule-skinner from Kansas. Fat, fifty and enterprising, she bustled about the store, gathering a dozen gowns of assorted design, toiled at the sewing machine and offered her comments.

"I call it a mortal shame, Jake Jarvis riggin' that pretty child in men's clothes all these years, and her workin' like a hard case ranch-hand."

159

"Read the note!" invited Lulu. She chuckled triumphantly and tossed the crumpled sheet. "See what he says? Hired a private teacher for Kate — some Omaha gent who's gonna make a lady of her. And she has to have a whole new wardrobe!"

"No expense spared, it says here," observed Ellie. "Never thought I'd live to see the day Jake Jarvis'd feel *that* way — about *anything*. He was always tight-fisted."

"Hats and slippers to match," enthused Lulu, waddling back and forth, rummaging energetically. Let's see now. A couple parasols for sure. Reticles. Gloves. Oh, happy day! This is gonna cost old Jake!"

"What size?" asked Ellie.

"Don't worry, I know her size," Lulu assured her. "The only decent gown that girl owns was bought right here in this store, and I swear her figure hasn't changed since then."

"She won't need no corsets, that's for sure," opined Ellie. "I recall she's trim around the middle."

"*I'll* decide about that — thanks for remindin' me," chuckled Lulu. "Three corsets — camisoles — all different colors — what a day this is gonna be . . . !"

A short time later, Lulu Duprez drove her surrey out of Hortonville at high speed, whipping her matched bays. The rear of the vehicle was jam-packed with the garments ordered by the Double J boss, and protected from the rising dust by a couple of sheets. Ellie had been left in charge of the store. The great project of outfitting Kate Jarvis warranted Lulu's personal attention; she intended having the last word as to what the beautiful blonde should wear, and was determined to exact payment from her cantankerous sire.

When Larry and Stretch sighted the stalled surrey, they were on their way back to the ranch headquarters, ambling their mounts out of a straggle of brush on Double J's south quarter.

The fat woman, red-faced and fearsome in her black bombazine, stood by the team, yelling abuse, gesticulating wildly.

"Looks like she needs help," Larry observed.

"Looks like," agreed Stretch. "But what d'you say we forget we seen her?" He grimaced nervously. "That's one scary female."

"Rigged like a lady," frowned Larry. "But cussin' them bays like a mule-skinner."

"You're just as spooked as me," accused Stretch.

"I ain't denyin' it," said Larry. "But she's a female in trouble." Grinning wryly, he nudged his mount to movement. "C'mon. I'll allow she's a wild one, but what the hell? We're two against one."

Lulu turned and waved eagerly as the riders came into view.

"Over here, boys!" she called. "Get a hustle on!"

They reined up on the trail,

dismounted and doffed their Stetsons.

"'Afternoon, ma'am." Larry greeted her with careful courtesy. "Somethin' we can do for you?"

"Double J riders, huh?" She noted the familiar brand on the ranch ponies. "Didn't know Jake Jarvis'd hired extra hands."

"We signed on for the drive to Omaha," explained Larry.

"Well, lucky I ran into you," she declared. "Double J is where I'm headed. Right-side teamer balked a couple minutes ago, and now he won't budge." She scowled belligerently at the nickering bay. "Goldurn stubborn critter!"

"Has to be a reason," opined Larry. He began checking the animal's hooves. "And here it is. A rock stuck in the frog. Left forehoof."

He fished out his jack-knife, while Stretch asked,

"In deep?"

"Just deep enough to make him balk," drawled Larry. "I figure he'll move easy enough, soon as I've dug it out."

"Best chance I ever had to do business with Jake Jarvis," fretted the fat woman, "and this pesky buzzard-bait had to slow me down."

"You ain't far from the ranch-house," Larry pointed out. "We'll get you there in ten minutes or less."

"Sure obliged to you boys," she acknowledged. "I'm Lulu Duprez — Madam Duprez to my customers." Gesturing to her cargo, she grinned and confided, "new gowns and stuff — for Kate. Your boss ordered 'em."

"Makes sense," Stretch commented. "I mean what's the use of him hirin' the dude to make a lady of her, if she don't *look* like a lady?"

"How about this teacher Jake hired?" she demanded. "Hey! He wouldn't be French, would he?"

"English," said Larry.

"English, huh?" she frowned. "A gentleman?"

"You might call him that," shrugged

Larry. "Leastways he can talk and act like a gentleman, and I got to admit he's teachin' her good."

"Already she's gettin' to talk high-falutin'," offered Stretch.

"Name of Roderick," said Larry.

"Roderick." She nodded thoughtfully. "All right, and what do I call you boys?"

"He's Stretch, I'm Larry." Larry finished his chore, prising out the offending stone and tossing it aside. "And this critter oughtn't give you any more trouble. Climb aboard, ma'am, and we'll escort you."

"Much obliged," said Lulu. "Gimme a boost, will you?"

She waddled to the front seat. They each grasped an elbow and, after much heaving and grunting, managed to raise her to the seat. She yelled to the team and flicked her reins, as the Texans remounted and turned their horses.

A shock was in store for the case-hardened nomads. They were inclined to believe they had seen and heard everything, until they reined up beside the surrey in front of the Double J ranch-house. An entirely different Lulu descended from the rig to be greeted by the runty rancher, his daughter and her tutor from the porch. She was graceful now, a lady of great poise and elegance, despite her formidable bulk. She acknowledged Jake's growled greeting with a sweet smile and a gentle nod.

"And good afternoon to you, Mister Jarvis," she cooed. "Pray pardon my tardiness. I should have arrived earlier, but for a small mishap." She turned to gesture to the Texans, whose jaws were sagging. "One of my animals had gone lame. Your new employees were most gallant. They were kind enough to remove an impediment from the poor creature's hoof."

"To do *what*?" frowned Jake.

"It was a rock," mumbled Stretch.

"Oh?" Jake shrugged impatiently. "Well, enough of this jawin'. Valentine,

Emerson, you tote that finery into the house. Mrs Duprez, this here is Mister Roderick from Omaha . . ."

"English, I believe?" smiled Lulu.

"Your servant, Madame Duprez," said Roderick.

"Ah, tres gallant!" she beamed. "And, soon, our dear Kate will be tres chic, nes pas?"

"Mais oui," smiled Roderick.

"All of sudden nobody's talking English!" Jake sourly complained. "C'mon, let's get on with this chore. I want to see Kate rigged ladylike."

The Texans unloaded Lulu's wares and toted them into the parlor, then loitered on the porch, trading comments with the ramrod, his spouse and Curly Becker.

"It's a day I've been waitin' for," Bessie Finlay told them. "Our Kate — dressed the way a girl *ought* to be dressed."

"I've always said Kate's a good-looker," remarked Finlay, draping an arm about his wife's shoulders. "Kind of like Bessie, back when I courted her."

"Jake's gettin' his money's worth out of the dude," opined Curly. "Got to hand it to that Roderick feller. He's taught Kate fast. I hear her talkin', and it just ain't the same. She sounds — different now."

"Like a lady," smiled Bessie. "And it's no more than she deserves."

"What's eatin' him?" asked Finlay, nodding to Stretch.

"I guess he's still tryin' to figure it out — and so am I," grinned Larry. "When we met up with Mrs Duprez, she was cussin' her team like an old mule-skinner from way back. Then we fetched her to the ranch and she started in talkin' like some high-born lady from back east."

"Somebody should've warned you about Lulu," chuckled Curly.

The fat woman's visit to Double J was a resounding success in more ways than one. Every gown was a perfect fit. One by one, they were modelled by

Kate, dressed by Lulu in her bedroom, then led into the parlor to be inspected and admired by her tutor and sire.

At her first appearance, her hair piled high and secured by a jewelled comb, her well-curved frame emphasized by a ball gown of blue silk that left her arms and shoulders bare, Jake signified his approval with an ear-splitting whoop, startling the Englishman and winning a complacent smile from Lulu.

"*That's* the one!" he yelled. "By thunder, when Mitch climbs offa that coach and sees her in that outfit, I swear he'll flop on his knees and propose right off — damned if he won't!"

"It would hardly be appropriate," protested Roderick. "This, Mister Jarvis, is a gown for evening wear, something for a special occasion, such as a grand ball, a reception . . . "

"But, damnitall, it'll be broad daylight when the stage arrives!" argued Jake. "And she never looked purtier in her whole doggone life!"

It took Lulu and the Englishman some little time to convince Jake that his daughter should not meet the westbound stage attired in a ball gown. At Roderick's suggestion, Lulu hustled Kate back to her bedroom. The ball gown was replaced by an outfit more suited to street wear, an eye-catching affair of deep red velvet, topped by an elegant chapeau festooned with lace and artificial flowers. When Jake saw this ensemble, he whooped again and loudly asserted,

"I sired the most beautiful gal in all Nebrasky — and I'll whup the man says I didn't!"

By the time the last gown had been shown, the little man was quivering with excitement, visualizing his daughter's easy conquest of the college-educated Mitch. How could Dan Firestone's son, or any other red-blooded buck of this territory, resist a girl so radiantly beautiful, so queenly, so fashionably dressed? He rendered the Englishman breathless by pounding his back and almost knocking him from his chair.

"You're doin' just fine, Roderick, by golly! We've won already — and we're gonna celebrate!"

A few moments later, as she bustled out of the house, Lulu Duprez was chuckling elatedly and stuffing a thick wad of cash into her reticle.

"The lot!" she bragged to the Texans. "Every last item! He bought it all — and paid cash!"

"Mighty profitable deal, huh Lulu?" grinned Curly, as he walked her to her waiting surrey.

"I am pleased," she loftily replied, "that your employer appreciates the quality of all merchandise available at my establishment."

The Texans boosted her up to the driver's seat. She thanked them with a cheery wave, then gathered her reins and yelled to the bays.

"*Giddap* — you lop-eared crow-bait . . . !"

Lulu Duprez's surrey was rolling away toward the town trail, when Kate emerged to be admired by the hired hands and their womenfolk, smiling and radiant in a flowing gown of flowered silk. The women heaved wistful sighs, while the men reverently bared their heads; it was as though they had witnessed a miracle.

"My father says," she graciously announced, "no more work today. And Curly should roast a side of beef. Tonight, we celebrate." Deke Finlay whooped and threw his hat in air, seized his spouse and swept her off her feet. Curly chuckled raspily and, in his sudden glee, performed a little jig. "And we won't have to send a rig to Hortonville for the liquid refreshment," added Kate, "because Pa says . . . "

"Whoo-eee!" yelled Curly.

"Pa says," finished Kate, "break out the Wild Mash!"

The reaction to this command intrigued Larry and Stretch. At the sound of those two words — Wild Mash — the men of Double J squared their shoulders and traded grins of anticipation. Their womenfolk shrugged resignedly and began eyeing the men askance, and the preparations got under way. The excitement was contagious; even the children were affected.

After offsaddling their horses and stowing their gear in the barn, the Texans surrendered to their curiosity and demanded an explanation. Curly obliged. They cornered him in his cook shack, where he labored willingly, cutting steaks and spare ribs, chuckling to himself.

"You sound like we're gonna celebrate Thanksgiving and Fourth of July and New Year's Eve all at the same time," observed Stretch. "What's it all about, Curly? What in tarnation is Wild Mash?"

"Some kind of booze?" challenged Larry.

"Somethin' special," Curly fervently assured them. "The kind of whiskey a drinkin' man dreams about. You can't buy it in no saloon. If the saloonkeepers could get their hands on the feller that cooks it up, I swear they'd lynch him. Why, we don't even know his real name! We call him Billy Moonlight, on account of nobody ever saw him in daylight. Always peddles his whiskey at night. Drives his wagon into this territory just twice a year, stops by every ranch and homestead, but stays far clear of town."

"And he'll always have customers," guessed Larry.

"Jake keeps his supply in the cellar, and keeps that cellar locked," grinned Curly. "You daren't pour Wild Mash into a regular glass. Hell, no. Glass'll crack every time. You have to drink it out of a tin cup. And Billy delivers it in coal-oil cans . . ."!

"Holy Hannah," frowned Stretch.

"You don't have to worry," said Curly. "Billy makes sure them cans is clean before he fills 'em. This is strong medicine I'm talkin' about, boys. Needs to be kept in steel. Nothin' else is strong enough to hold it. When he first started up in business — nobody knows where he built his still — Billy tried storin' it in stone jugs."

"You ain't gonna tell us his Wild Mash'd melt stone," Stretch protested.

"It didn't melt them stone jugs," said Curly. "It blew 'em up! And, when he tried regular whiskey kegs, it splintered 'em!"

"You're joshin' us," accused Stretch.

"This is the gospel I'm tellin' you," declared Curly.

"When Jake pours your share, you add water, savvy? You never tasted finer whiskey than Billy Moonlight's Wild Mash, but I'm warnin' you it ain't wise to take it straight. You cut it with water 'less you aim to stay drunk all week."

By sundown, Double J's celebration was beginning, and Russ Webb was idling his pony past the Glory Hole and on toward the thick brush west of the ranch headquarters. The pudgy hard case craved a private parley with the man known as English Eddie, and was willing to bide his time and await his chance.

Simultaneously, Brett Hawley and Gus Millane were spelling their horses on the flats east of the county seat, gazing toward the lights of Hortonville and planning their next move.

6

Warning From a Marauder

"WE'LL need a place to stay," drawled Hawley. He helped himself to a cigar from Millane's vest pocket and snapped his fingers. "Light."

"Damn you, Hawley," scowled Millane, as he scratched a match. "I've had my bellyful of you."

"You need me, so don't give me no arguments." Hawley puffed the cigar to life and nodded complacently. "Best we move into town, get us a room in a hotel. I don't plan on campin' out."

"We don't know why old Jarvis hired Roderick," Millane complained. "What kind of work would he be good for — on a cattle spread? That's what I don't understand."

"So maybe Roderick ain't at Double J,"

shrugged Hawley. "Maybe we'll find him right there in town. First we check into a hotel, then I start lookin' around You're totin' plenty dinero, so we'll make it a high-class hotel, huh?"

"I can't take a chance on Roderick sighting me," said Millane, "before I sight him."

"He'd recognize you for sure," nodded Hawley. "But he don't know me so good, so I reckon it's safe enough for me to move around this burg."

"Listen, if you start asking questions . . . ."

"You think I'm a fool? I ain't about to ask questions, tinhorn. I'll just use my ears. Bound to be talk about a stranger like Roderick, him with his fine clothes and his high-falutin' manners. All I have to do is listen. And, pretty soon, I'll know where to find him."

"I'd as soon we handled it quietly," muttered the gambler. "I don't relish the prospect of trying to outride a law-posse. A killing in broad daylight — a gunshot alerting the whole damn town.

There has to be an easier way — a quiet way."

"We might get lucky," grinned Hawley. "Might figure a way to make it look like an accident."

For his Hortonville headquarters, the burly ex-convict chose the McQuade House, a hotel located next door to one of the busiest banks, the Settlers Trust. Hawley insisted on a second floor double overlooking the main stem, ordered the gambler to retire, then demanded spending money and moved out to look the town over and begin his quest for information.

Within the hour, he had learned all he needed to know. Lulu Duprez had talked long and loud upon her return from Double J, and now it seemed three-quarters of the townfolk were discussing Little Jake's project, a private tutor to school his daughter in the social graces, a brand-new wardrobe.

While waiting on Hawley at the Palace Saloon, Gates the barkeep good-humoredly remarked,

"She'll be quite a sight to see, next time she comes to town."

"Meanin' this gal I keep hearin' of," guessed Hawley. "Every place I go, I hear folks talkin' about — what's her name again?"

"Kate Jarvis — Little Jake's daughter," offered Gates. "Took that sawn-off old heller a long time to make up his mind, seems to me. I tell you, all the years I've been tendin' bar in Hortonville, I've scarce ever seen Kate rigged female. Always rigged out like a workin' cowpoke, you know? Talks like one too."

"Well . . . " Hawley took a pull at his whiskey and shrugged unconcernedly, "I guess anybody can change."

"As well as lookin' like a lady, she's gonna talk like one," grinned the barkeep. "The way I hear it, Jake fetched this dude back from Omaha, some English jasper name of Roderick."

"And he's schoolin' the lady," mused Hawley.

"That's about the size of it," nodded

Gates. "And now we're all gettin' curious, wonderin' how she'll look — all prettied up."

He moved along the bar to serve other customers, leaving Hawley to finish his drink and survey his reflection in the mirror atop the shelves.

'Right here in town would be as good a place as any,' he assured himself. 'Too risky, tryin' to reach him at Double J. He'd be stickin' close to the house. Better to wait till the Jarvis girl comes to town. When she comes in, he'll likely tag along.'

As he strolled back toward the McQuade House, he passed a derby-hatted, check-suited individual tacking a poster to a wall. The poster proclaimed, in bright print, that the famous Overton Repertory Company would be coming to Hortonvile in the near future to present 'the 3-Act Drama LOST IN THE STORM — the brilliant presentation acclaimed by thousands during its triumphant tour of the territories west of Chicago!'

"Tell your friends," urged the man in the checkered suit. "And join the line outside the Horton Opera House when we start selling tickets. You wouldn't want to miss it, cowboy. An experience you'll never forget!"

"Yeah, sure," grunted Hawley.

He continued on his way, disinterested in the spruiker's remarks. Brett Hawley, thief, killer and ex-convict, was not exactly a patron of the arts. He had never heard of a play entitled Lost In The Storm nor of a group of traveling theatricals called the Overton Repertory. Neither, for that matter, had the sheriff of Horton County, nor any citizen of this territory.

But Sheriff Amos Trager might have worked up some interest, had he suspected there was no such organization as the Overton Repertory.

★ ★ ★

At Double J the celebration was well and truly under way. By the light of lamps hung above the ranchhouse porch and the glow of the barbecue fire, the hired hands danced with their womenfolk to music supplied by Stretch, a handy man with a guitar, and Little Jake, a fiddler of no mean talent. While the rancher stamped and fiddled and whooped, Finlay and the other hands whirled the ladies and made merry. Generous shots of the notorious Wild Mash were poured into tin cups and passed around, after which the festivities became noisier. The small fry, straddling a top rail of the near corral, feasted on spare ribs and yelled encouragement to their whooping parents.

"Here's your share — take it gentle!" warned Curley, confronting Larry and thrusting a brimming mug at him. "I already cut it for you. Half Wild Mash — half water."

The chuck-boss scuttled back to his fire. Larry, squatting in a caneback on the porch, squinted into his drink and traded comments with Roderick, who

183

was perched on the porch-rail, puffing a cigar and watching the dancers. The Englishman had been served his share a short time before; his tin cup was almost empty.

"This'll be the first time I ever drank watered whiskey — willingly," Larry declared.

"Great stuff, I assure you," offered Roderick. "Didn't quite know what to expect — until I sampled it. Quite deceptive actually. Delicate Bouquet. Out of character with — ah — the rather acid taste. But good stuff."

Larry took a stiff swig, gulped it down and shook his head dazedly. With his eyes watering, he remarked,

"I don't know what it's got — but it's sure got *somethin'*."

"Has the most extraordinary effect, by gad," muttered Roderick. "Stimulates the versatility."

"Does what?" Larry asked, blinking dubiously. "Listen, all I feel is hot inside — like I've been drinkin' fire."

"Your tall friend, for instance."

Roderick sipped another mouthful, while Larry marveled at his perfect balance, wondering why he didn't topple from the rail. "Vershal — verse — talented feller, your friend. Able to play two guitars sim — simmum — simmle — both at the same time."

"That's crazy," growled Larry. "No man can play on two guitars at the same time." He glanced toward his partner. "He only got one guitar anyway."

"I have perfect sight, Mister Valentine," countered Roderick. "I assure you — your friend is performing on two guitars."

"Look closer," challenged Larry. "Count how many guitars he's holdin'."

"Confound it, you're right." Roderick focussed on the guitar and Stretch's busy hands, then raised his gaze a mite. "but now — damnitall — he appears to have acquired an extra head!"

"You're drunk," accused Larry. "Crazy drunk and seein' double."

"On the contrar-rary — never felt

better!" chuckled Roderick. "Ah, my friend, to be part of this gathering of humble but lovable colonials — reminds me of old times — the great occasions — the grand balls." He sighed wistfully and took another pull at his drink. "Gad, how I miss the old country — dear Mother England. You may recall — I believe I mentioned my father, Sir Nigel Roderick . . ."

"Drink your booze and tell your wild lies," Larry invited, "if it keeps you happy."

"I remember a grand brawl at the palace . . ." began Roderick.

"They got a Palace Saloon in England, just like in Hortonvile?" interjected Larry. "And who started the brawl anyway?"

"Brawl? What brawl? I refer, sir, to the grand ball at the palace — meaning Buckingham Palace."

"A *big* saloon, huh? Dancin' as well as booze and games of chance . . . ?"

"*Not* a saloon! I say, Valentine old chap, that's a bit thick. How could you compare the home of our gracious Queen Victoria with a — a common gaming house? How could you become so confused?"

"It's easy — when you're drinkin' Billy Moonlight's Wild Mash."

"*I'm* not confused," bragged Roderick. "I was only a youngster at the time, but I remember how proud I felt, attending the Prince Consort's birthday ball with my father and brother — poor, dear Cedric. That never-to-be-forgotten moment when my father — Sir Nigel you know — actually danced with her Majesty — while the orchestra played a Welsh shorts."

"Played what?"

"A Strauss waltz. Confound you, Valentine, is the liquor affecting your hearing?"

"I hear fine. It's you, Ed. You're talkin' funny."

"On the contrar-rary, my diction is perfect."

"Well, I know what I heard, and I'm thinkin' that must've been some wild

187

party — what with all them Welsh musicians playin' in their shorts. And all them fine women to see 'em."

"Valentine . . . " Roderick turned slightly, the better to focus on Larry, "trying to converse with you is a diffle — diffit — impossible task. It's as though — we speak a different language."

"No use blamin' Texans," growled Larry, "just because everybody else is a doggone foreigner."

"Shall we join the ladies?" Observing that Kate was emerging from the house, radiant in one of her new gowns, the Englishman slid from the rail. Mildly surprised to discover he had flopped to his knees, he struggled upright, adjusted his cravat and smoothed his hair. "I see our beautiful hostess has deigned to join us. I must, of course, request the honor of dancing with her. How about you, Valentine?"

"No, thanks, Ed," said Larry. "I don't wanta dance with you. Better you should dance with Kate."

"You're confused again," accused Roderick.

"You too," opined Larry.

"I? Never." Roderick squared his shoulders. "I'm an English gentleman, the son of a baronet, and I'll have you know we Rodericks know how to hold our liquor."

"Yeah, I can see that," nodded Larry. "But you oughta let go of that booze before you ask Kate to dance."

Suddenly aware he still held his drink, Roderick drained his cup and tossed it away, aiming for the yard. Larry ducked, because the cup flew in the opposite direction, clattering against the wall behind him. He swore bitterly and accused Roderick of being drunk.

"Dunk be drammed," the Englishman retorted. "I assure you I'm as sober as a jug. And now . . . " He smiled in anticipation and began moving along the porch toward the fair Kate, "If Mister Jarvis can play a waltz . . . "

"Not in his Long Johns," begged Larry.

Roderick managed to fight off his fatigue and maintain his balance long enough to escort Kate down the steps. Responding to his request, Jake scratched a mite lower and Stretch managed a three-quarter time beat. Applauded by their over-stimulated audience, the beautiful pupil and her handsome tutor waltzed a circuit of the yard, while Larry plucked up his courage and gulped two more mouthfuls of Wild Mash. The hired hands joined the waltz, one of them forgetting to bring his wife. Larry lurched up from his chair, moved cautiously to the edge of the porch and leaned against the rail, watching the dancers.

"Jake must've sent out invites all across the territory," he reflected. "Must be fifty-sixty people dancin' down there. Won't be enough Wild Mash to go round."

That one circuit of the yard was

as much as Roderick could manage. With his senses reeling and his vision blurring, he mumbled a compliment and a plea to be excused and surrendered his fair partner to Curly Becker, who bellowed to his boss to play faster. The dancers were whirling and whooping again, when the Englishman began a discreet retreat.

Convinced he might collapse at any moment or — worse still — become violently ill, Roderick stumbled away from the scene of revelry. He had a vague notion of steering a course for the privvies out back of the ranch buildings, but his ability to navigate was seriously impaired by Billy Moonlight's famous product; he kept right on stumbling.

After a few minutes, the chill of the night breeze cleared his head slightly. He found himself moving faster. A backward glance indicated he had retreated a fair distance from the Double J headquarters.

'So much the better,' he decided. 'Can't — disgrace myself — before these hard-drinking yokels. Better they don't see me.'

What lay ahead? Blinking dazedly to the west he noted the clump of brush. The night breeze smote him again. He shuddered, reeled a few paces, then righted himself and resumed his stumbling. By the time he was moving out of the moonlight with the brush tugging at his clothes, he was footsore and groggy again, barely able to keep his eyes open. The grass in the small clearing proved to be cool and soft. He flopped gratefully, but manfully resisted the urge in his pockets for a cigar. And then, despite his reduced condition, he clearly heard the sound close by, a horse nickering. The second sound, a man's mumbled curse, caused him to call a challenge.

"Who's there?"

He had a blurred impression of a shadowy figure moving into the clearing. Webb had taken the precaution of drawing his bandana up to his eyes, though the gloom was intense;

Roderick's chances of identifying him were one in a thousand.

"Never mind who I am, Ed Roderick," he muttered. "I know who *you* are. And that ain't *all* I know."

"You have the advantage . . . " began Roderick.

"Damn right I got the advantage." Webb chuckled triumphantly. "And information, Roderick. Yes siree, I got important information. But it's gonna cost you — savvy?"

"I haven't the — vaguest notion . . . "

"You're drunk!"

"Never! Slightly tipsy — but in full possession of my facul . . . " Roderick took a deep breath, then carefully pronounced the word. "Faculties."

"Meanin' you hear what I'm sayin'?" challenged Webb. "I got no time to waste, mister. If you're too likkered-up to savvy what I'm talkin' about, I'll have to wait and . . . "

"I understand you," Roderick curtly assured him. "And — I say! Are you suffering from toothache?" he squinted perplexedly. "Your face appears to be wrapped in — some kind of bandage?"

"Shuddup and listen!" ordered Webb.

"Must you be so infernally rude?" protested Roderick. "Are there *no* gentlemen in this God-forsaken wilderness?"

"If you value your life, you'd better heed what I'm about to tell you!"

"Good Lord!"

"I want cash, understand. A thousand dollars."

"You intend robbing me? Prepos — preposterous! The small change in my pockets would hardly . . . "

"Mister, I ain't talkin' about nickels and dimes. I mean real money. A thousand I said. That's my price — for what I'm sellin'."

"And — exactly what are you trying to sell, my good man?"

"I know somethin' *you* need to know. I know you've been set up."

"Set up?" Roderick grimaced in exasperation. "What does that mean, may I ask? If you'd explain in plain

English, instead of adhering to the meaningless jargon of this desolate frontier . . . "

"Somebody plans on killin' you, Roderick."

"Killing — *me*? You speak of — murder . . . ?"

"That's the word, boy. Murder it's gonna be, if they catch up with you. I'm givin' it to you straight. I heard 'em makin' their plans. I know who they are and why they want you dead. But that's all I'm sayin' for now. I don't name 'em till I collect."

"But this is ridiculous! What possible reason could they have for . . . ?"

"That's somethin' else I'm sellin', Roderick. Their names — and the reasons."

Roderick bowed his head and began stroking his temples, the while he struggled to make sense of the marauder's assertions. In vain he protested he had no way of acquiring a thousand dollars. Webb retorted he could beg, borrow or steal it.

"I don't much care *how* you get it, just so long as you're ready to pay me off next time I look you up."

"When — where . . . ?"

"I ain't sayin'. But don't wait too long, Roderick. Your time is runnin' out."

"Most preposterous thing I've ever heard."

"It's the truth. You can't afford to take a chance I'm lyin', Roderick. The way it adds up, you got only one hope of stayin' alive. You have to know their names — and their reasons. A man can protect himself, if he knows his enemies. But, if he *don't* know 'em, he's wide open — an easy target — a dead pigeon." The marauder's voice was becoming fainter. For a moment, Roderick feared the whiskey had affected his hearing. Then he realized the speaker was moving away from him, slinking back into the brush, still talking. "You have to know their names, Roderick. And I'll tell you — for a thousand. Get that thousand. Get it . . . "

Roderick squatted in silence, stroking his temples, wondering if his imagination were playing tricks. When, from somewhere west of the brush, he heard the receding hoofbeats of a fast-moving horse, he was forced to conclude his nocturnal visitor had been real, moving like a shadow and trying to peddle a far-fetched story for the sake of earning an easy $1000, but real enough.

"Practical joker," he decided, lurching to his feet. "Most ridiculous story I've ever heard. An assassination plot — against *me*? What rot! Absolute drivel."

By the time he returned to the brightly-lit area in front of the ranch-house, the party was dying, the merry-makers wilting somewhat. Two hours of energetic dancing to Little Jake's feverish fiddling, plus one whole can of Wild Mash, was as much as the hardiest hell-raiser could manage. From the porch, a clear-eyed and serene Kate delivered a short speech of thanks to her well-wishers; she was in fine condition for doing so, having wisely abstained from Billy Moonlight's brain-shaking booze.

The weary ranch-hands returned to their cabins with their women and children, after Little Jake had extinguished the lamps and announced the close of the festivities. The rancher and his daughter retired to their rooms, closely followed by Roderick, who barely managed to locate his quarters. The Englishman fell asleep while removing his coat, sinking slowly to the floor beside his bed. Curly Becker made it to the bunkhouse — on all fours. Stretch, though close to collapse, observed that the barbecue fire still burned bright. Fearing the wind might scatter sparks, determined to save Double J from being burned to the ground, he summoned up the strength to draw a pail of water from the well and douse the cook-fire. Grinning smugly at his partner, he remarked,

"Just as well *one* of us stayed sober,

kept his wits about him and used his eyes."

"You're no sober-rer than me," scoffed Larry. "And I know how *I* feel . . . "

"Takes more'n a couple shots of Wild Mash to put *me* down," bragged Stretch.

He turned toward the bunkhouse, yawned and stretched and filled his lungs with the clean night air, then fell flat on his face. Larry performed the herculean feat of raising him from his prone position, draping him across his shoulders and toting him all the way to the bunkhouse. Negotiating his formidable burden through the doorway proved difficult; he gave up on trying to carry Stretch through, let him crumple to the threshold, then hauled him to his bunk by a leg. And that was as much as he remembered until 8.30 of the following morning.

The sun rose on schedule, but was ignored by the people of Double J. Nobody opened an eye before 7.15.

Larry came to his senses and immediately regretted it. He found himself sprawled on his back in the middle of the bunkhouse floor, fully dressed, his Stetson wedged tight about his ears. He got rid of his headgear, humbly grateful that, when he tugged it off, his head stayed on his shoulders. Groaning a curse, he raised himself to a sitting posture and blinked at his partner. Stretch was coming alive, but slowly, painfully; he lay on the floor beside his bunk.

For a long moment, they eyed each other.

"Some sonofabitch been stompin' on my head — all night," the taller Texan complained. "Leastways that's how it feels."

If I'm never gonna feel any better'n I feel right now," declared Larry, "I might's well shoot myself."

"I'd offer to do it for you," sighed Stretch, "only I'm too weak to pull a gun." He sat up, winced in anguish and held his hands to his ears. "What's that thunder?"

"Couldn't be thunder," mumbled Larry. "Not in broad daylight." He squinted toward the open doorway. "Sounds like a steer broke from the herd, and now he's headed straight in here."

"That's no itty bitty steer!" groaned Stretch. "Gotta be a buffalo!"

It was neither a steer nor a buffalo. It was Curly Becker, and he wasn't tramping. In his bare feet, pallid and hollow-eyed, he tiptoed into the bunkhouse. He toted a tray containing two steaming mugs and he was trembling, so that the mugs made a clattering sound; Larry was sure that clattering sound could be heard as far away as the Kansas Border.

"If you gents — drink this," Curly whispered, setting the tray down, "maybe you won't feel like killin' yourselves after all."

"What're you tryin' to feed us?" Larry asked softly.

"For pity's sake don't *shout*!" begged Curly.

"I ain't shoutin!" hissed Larry.

"This here is — what Billy Moonlight calls the antidote," explained Curly. "Every place he sells his booze, he tells folks how to mix up this stuff. Only way to get you back on your feet." As Larry moved a shaking hand to reach a mug, he warned, "it tastes gosh-awful, but it's a real life-saver."

"I can work up the nerve, if you can," whispered Stretch, reaching for the other mug.

"Don't sip it," chided Curly. "Just hold your nose and gulp it all down."

They obeyed, then dropped the empty mugs, clasped at their bellies and began coughing frantically.

"What's in it?" gasped Stretch.

"Oh, a whole lotta stuff," said the chuck-boss. "Cayenne pepper and ketchup, couple slugs of brandy and a little vinegar. A dab of molasses. All kindsa stuff. Don't worry. You'll feel better in a little while. Why, five minutes after I fed him his antidote, Mister Roderick fetched his razor and headed for the spring over yonder of the vegetable patch."

"Gonna cut his throat," guessed Stretch.

"He's got the right idea," opined Larry.

"Hell, no." Curly managed a feeble apology of a grin. "He's just gonna shave and wash up."

"Cold water might do it," Larry suggested to Stretch, as he struggled upright.

"Strip buck naked and flop right in?" frowned Stretch.

"Worst that could happen is we'd drown," said Larry.

"Okay by me," sighed Stretch, fighting to get perpendicular. "I'd as soon drown than go on feelin' so poorly."

They spoke softly to the chuck-boss, thanking him for fetching the antidote. He said don't mention it, but for pity's sake don't shout, and crept back to the cook-shack. After some rummaging, they located their shaving gear and found soap and towels.

Out into the glaring sunlight they tottered, their eyes streaming. They steered a ragged course for the natural bathing facilities available to Double J's male employees, a pool screened from view of the house by high grass and thick brush.

They found the Englishman, standing by a tree to which he had attached a mirror. He was shaving, working his razor with care, a damp towel knotted about his midriff.

"I bathed," he announced, as they paused to squint at him. "Must say it helps. I may survive after all. Water is deuced chilly."

"Yeah, okay," mumbled Stretch, unbuckling his gunbelt. "Listen, if you cut your throat, don't bleed in our bathwater."

"A gruesome thought," said Roderick.

Somewhat laboriously, the Texans peeled off their clothes. They stood at the edge of the pool a long moment, summoning their courage. Then, stiffly, like a couple of severed trees, they keeled forward and fell in, striking the surface with a resounding splash, sinking. Roderick froze with his razor poised, staring solemnly at the troubled water and wondering if the intrepid nomads had made a suicide pact. But no. After a few moments, they surfaced, spluttering, gasping.

They floundered to the edge of the pool, groped for their soap and began a pretence of enjoying their bath, while the Englishman finished shaving and donned his clothes.

Later, while they were towelling their battle-scarred bodies, he squatted at the base of the tree and drawled a comment.

"Quite a party, what?"

"Ed, if it's all the same to you, we'd as soon forget it ever happened," growled Stretch.

Having donned pants, boots and

undershirts, the Texans decided they had a better than even chance of shaving without inflicting fatal gashes. They began, while Roderick talked on.

"Had the most extraordinary experience last night. Became a trifle thick-headed, you know. Desperately in need of fresh air. Managed to reach the brush." He gestured languidly toward the brush. "Must have fainted — or fallen asleep. I suppose it had to be a nightmare a bizarre dream."

"Dreamed you were dancin' with Prince Albert again, huh?" challenged Larry lathering his stubbled cheeks.

"You misunderstand," sighed Roderick. "It was my father, Sir Nigel, who danced at Buckingham Palace. And not with the Prince Consort. With the Queen herself, I'm proud to say."

"Okay, Ed, tell us what you dreamed about, if you got nothin' better to do," offered Stretch.

"But *was* it a dream?" frowned Roderick.

"Now he's gonna argue — with himself," complained Larry.

"I mean, it was all so clear," declared Roderick. "Almost pitch dark, come to think of it, but I seem to recall — quite distinctly — most of his face wrapped in a scarf. Heard his horse also."

"Who?" prodded Larry.

"The man who spoke to me," said Roderick. "Some outlandish poppycock about my life being in peril. An assassination plot. Confound his impudence, he demanded a thousand dollars!"

"For what?" frowned Larry.

"For revealing the identity of — whoever they are," shrugged Roderick. "The anonymous schemers planning my demise."

"Howzat again?" grunted Stretch.

"He means — whoever's figurin' on killin' him," explained Larry.

"One thousand dollars he demanded," nodded Roderick, "for naming them — and for revealing their motive. Well, of course, it's quite absurd.

How could anybody profit from my death? I'm penniless and, in this country, a nonentity. Who could profit by my demise? The whole idea is preposterous." He got to his feet and began moving off. "I'll dismiss it from my mind, eat a hearty breakfast and resume my duties. Au revoir, my friends."

After the Englishman returned to the Ranch-house, the Texans finished shaving, donned their upper garments and strapped on their hardware,

"Sure dreams wild, don't he?" Stretch remarked. "Must've been that crazy booze."

"Maybe," frowned Larry. "But let's you and me mosey over to the brush anyway. If some snooper *was* talkin' to the dude, he had to leave tracks."

They found the tell-tale marks, bootprints and track of a horse leading away from the brush as far as a strip of dusty ground, where the wind had swept clean. As they trudged to the mess-shack, wondering if they could work up an appetite, Larry flatly declarerd,

"He didn't dream it. He heard what he thought he heard. Somebody wants him dead — and I'd admire to know why."

7

Thieves' Council

BY early afternoon of that day, Little Jake was fully recovered from the celebration and eager to take Kate to town.

"To me, she looks just fine," he told Roderick. "But now I hanker to see how the townfolks take to her."

"A test?" challenged the Englishman. "You feel the time has come for her debut as a lady of fashion?"

"Meanin' what?" frowned Jake.

"You want to show me off, that's about the size of it," Kate good-humoredly accused.

"Anythin' wrong with that?" countered Jake. "I'll have one of the boys hitch a team to the surrey and we'll travel in rightaway." Eyeing Roderick intently, he growled a warning. "If anybody laughs at her — if folks don't show respect — you'll be all through. I'll know you done failed me."

"I have not failed you, sir," declared Roderick. "I predict the good citizens of Hortonville will be favorably impressed — and I assure you nobody will laugh at Miss Kate."

"She can buy herself another bonnet at Lulu's place," Jake decided. "We'll stay in town for supper, likely eat at Ravello's."

"One of the better restaurants, I presume." Roderick nodded knowingly. "You're anxious to study reactions to the lady's table manners."

"Like I been tellin' you right along," said Jake. "She has to *act* ladylike — in every way. Lookin' purty ain't enough."

A short time later, when the rancher emerged from the house, the surrey was waiting out front. Curly, Deke Finlay and the other hands had returned to their chores, but Larry and Stretch were sitting their mounts beside the surrey team, smoking, waiting patiently. Jake scowled at them and growled a challenge — just where the hell did they think they were going?

In a few terse sentences, Larry repeated Roderick's story of his encounter with a marauder.

"And he didn't dream it," he assured Jake. "We know, on account of we found track of the jasper that warned him."

"Warned him somebody's gunnin' for him?" frowned Jake.

"Don't forget we were ambushed on our way back from Omaha," said Larry.

"And don't forget the first bullet was triggered at Ed," drawled Stretch.

"Wouldn't be smart, you takin' Kate and him to town," declared Larry, "with no bodyguard."

Roderick was escorting Kate from the house now. Frowning at them over his shoulder, the little man shrugged impatiently and climbed up to the driver's seat.

"I could leave the dude behind, but I'd as soon he come along," he muttered. "Got to admit she looks better — escorted by him — than taggin' around with me."

"You're as handsome as Ed, Jake," said Stretch, poker-faced. "But in a different way."

"Button your lip," snapped Jake. "And keep your eyes peeled."

The party encountered no mishap during the journey to the county seat; the excitement began when Jake stalled the rig out front of the Bon Ton. Curious locals hovered close to watch Roderick help Kate from the surrey. She was looking her best, bearing little resemblance to the hoyden in blue jeans so familiar to the citizens of Hortonville. The gay chapeau, furled parasol and figure-hugging gown caused a flurry of enthusiasm that soon became a riot.

Their curiosity aroused by the crush of townfolk surging about the surrey, a quartet of Hammerhead cowpokes began forcing their way through. Local layabouts, gamblers and farm-hands joined the throng and, in a matter of moments, Larry and Stretch were dropping from their mounts and bellowing to the struggling men to stay clear; Jake was cursing luridly while wild-eyed men jostled one another in their eagerness to reach the smiling Kate.

"Quit smilin'!" the little man chided. "You're drivin' 'em wilder'n Billy Moonlight's booze!"

Attempting to remonstrate with a heavy-breathing cowpoke, Roderick was backhanded and sent reeling. Another half-dozen hot-blooded locals joined the crush and the team-horses neighed in alarm; the rig was almost overturned.

Watching from the opposite sidewalk, Brett Hawley and Gus Millane traded glances.

"Might be the best chance yet," Hawley quietly remarked, his hand on the hilt of the knife sheathed at his belt. "Easy to get close to him. And I'd be free and clear before they found his carcass."

"It's building up to quite a ruckus," observed Millane.

About to step off the sidewalk, Hawley abruptly changed his mind. Amos Trager, Horton County's aging but durable sheriff, was advancing on the rioters from the downtown area, the blond and bulky Bloomfeld lumbering in his wake. Both lawmen had drawn their Colts and were yelling reprimands.

While Larry helped Roderick to his feet, Stretch positioned himself in front of Kate and her runty sire and began discouraging her too-eager admirers. The taller Texan didn't much mind if the towners and cowpokes stared at her, but keenly disapproved their efforts to maul her. His chivalrous instincts aroused, he clobbered a wild-eyed ranch-hand and growled a reproach.

"Look as much as you want — but no pawin'!"

Trager and Bloomfeld arrived, bellowing commands that fell on deaf ears. By lashing out with their six-guns, the Texans managed to clear a path for Kate, her father and the Englishman, ushering them to the doorway of the Bon Ton, where Lulu Duprez screamed abuse at the rioters.

The lawmen, struggling to manacle a couple of over-stimulated cowpokes, traded worried frowns.

"Worst fracas I can recall, Olaf!" panted Trager. "Damn and blast — how much longer can it last?"

"Little Jake's fault," mumbled the deputy. "He brought some fancy female to town — and the boys're goin' wild."

"Great day in the mornin'!" Trager had caught a glimpse of the laughing girl being hustled into the Bon Ton. "That's Jake's gal — young Kate!"

The locals were surging toward the store entrance; Lulu was slamming the door in their faces, when somebody yelled,

"Fire!"

Suddenly the rioters were distracted — the lawmen also. All eyes turned toward the billowing smoke rising from behind the Settlers Trust Bank a half-block uptown.

"Must be the old Patton warehouse!" Bloomfeld bellowed in Trager's ear. "Didn't I say that place was a fire-trap? Should've been torn down years ago!"

"Hey — ain't that . . . ?" Trager pointed excitedly. "Ain't that Horrie Puckeridge — from the bank . . . ?"

The manager of the Settlers Trust had emerged from the bank and was beckoning urgently, a hand clasped to his head, blood streaming down his face.

"The hell with these no-accounts," muttered Trager, unhitching his keyring. The befuddled rioters, relieved of their manacles, scuttled away, while the lawmen barged uptown to the bank with the locals hustling after them. Puckeridge, a lean veteran with ash-grey hair, was slumped against a porch-post, dabbing at his bloodied head.

"Nathan — the cashier . . . " he gasped, as the lawmen reached him.

"Inside. Hurt — still unconscious. And a customer — Tom Gates — the barkeep — dead. Three men in dusters and masks — cleaned out the safe. One of them — clubbed me — and Nathan. Gates tried to struggle with another. He was — stabbed."

"Which way . . . ?" began Bloomfeld.

"When I came to my senses," sighed the banker, "they were making for the rear door. They — took my keys . . . "

"Arm yourselves!" Trager roared at the locals. "I want this whole block surrounded . . . !"

"Too late," groaned Puckeridge. "It .happened — almost five minutes ago . . . "

"They were ridin' out while we had our hands full!" raged Bloomfeld. The usually placid deputy, half-Jewish, half-Swedish, had numbered barkeep Gates among his close friends. "Made their getaway — damn 'em to hell — while we were tryin' to break up that riot!"

"Consider yourselves sworn in!" The sheriff gestured urgently. "I'll take as many as can get armed and mounted inside five minutes! Two posses! Olaf's party'll scout the area east and south. I'll take my bunch west — then north. Get a move on, men!"

Slumped on a sidewalk bench, Hawley and the gambler watched the exodus of angry riders. The two blocks so busy a short time before were almost deserted, when the blanket-covered body of the barkeep was carried out of the Settlers Trust. A few moments later, Doc Dudley arrived to attend Puckeridge and his cashier. On the other side of the alley behind the bank, volunteer fire-fighters began a half-hearted effort to save the abandoned Patton warehouse; already the building was almost gutted.

"Someone got lucky," Hawley remarked, helping himself to a cigar from the gambler's pocket. He snapped his fingers. "A light, tinhorn." Millane gave him a match. He scratched it to life and got his cigar working. "Somebody picked a helluva time to hit that bank.

Smart work. Real professional job."

"I'm more concerned with Roderick," said Millane, glancing furtively toward the Bon Ton. "And I'm wondering how long he'll stay in town."

"He ain't apt to leave rightaway," drawled Hawley. "Meanwhile, it might be smarter if we watch that store from the window of our room. Get a good enough view from there."

As they rose to their feet, Little Jake appeared in the doorway of the Bon Ton, his harsh voice raised in a yell that echoed all along the block. A stablehand scuttled out of a nearby livery and came hustling toward him.

"Tend my team!" Jake ordered him. "Take the rig back to the barn. I want it ready to roll again — nine-thirty tonight." He gestured impatiently to Larry's sorrel and Stretch's pinto. "Better stable them critters too."

"Yessir, Mister Jarvis," nodded the stablehand. "Hey, Miss Kate sure looks purty. Bet you're proud of her."

The rancher grinned smugly, fished

out a coin and tossed it to be caught deftly by the stablehand.

"That's for noticin', Jerry."

As they sauntered to the hotel, Hawley nudged Millane and opined.

"If the old man's stayin', you can bet the panhandler'll stay too."

They passed the bank, paused in the entrance to the narrow alley separating it from the McQuade House and, for a few moments, watched the fire-fighters at work. There was a hurried scatter when the roof of the old warehouse collapsed. Moving on, Hawley and the gambler entered the lobby to find the desk-clerk trying to placate a couple of indignant guests. One Hawley recognized as the check-suited jasper tacking up posters for the Overton Repertory. The other he also recognized, a well-dressed redhead who eyed the clerk sternly and declared,

"I'm just as indignant, just as shocked, as Mister Avery here. Came to this town to canvass your local ranches, hoping to buy beef for my Chicago connections . . . "

"Please, Mister Dangar, don't think of checking out now," begged the clerk. "Horton County ranchers raise the best cattle in the territory. As for you, Mister Avery . . . "

"Listen, feller, if you think a company as important as the Overton Repertory is gonna perform in a town like this," blustered Avery, "a hell-town — with street-fights and . . . "

"A fire — robbery and murder," frowned Dangar. "Next door to this very hotel! Damnitall, a visitor just isn't *safe* . . . "

"And me thinking Hortonville was a law and order town," complained Avery.

"Take my word for it," said the clerk. "All this violence is — is out of character — in this fine, peace-loving community."

"Peace-loving, he calls it," gibed Avery. "A riot and a fire, a robbery and a murder . . . "

"You cancelling, Mister Avery?" asked Dangar.

"I'll wire the boss, have the company change the itinerary," nodded Avery. "Safer if they swing south and play the river towns."

"I urge you to reconsider," frowned the clerk.

"Only service you can do for me and my associate is reserve passage on the next stage out," growled Dangar.

"That goes for me and Mister Wiggins as well," declared Avery.

"Very well, gentlemen." The clerk shrugged resignedly, while Millane glanced sidelong at Hawley, wondering at his obvious interest in the tall redhead. "But there won't be a coach through Hortonville until eleven o'cock tomorrow. The east-bound."

"That'll suit me fine," said Dangar.

"And me," nodded Avery. "I guess Omaha's a damn sight safer than this hell-town."

Dangar and Avery quit the lobby by way of the alcove leading into the ground-floor passage, neither of them sparing a backward glance for Hawley and his companion.

"Red didn't even notice me," Hawley said softly. "But I sure remember *him*."

"What . . . ?" began Millane.

"Remember I talked of an old buddy of mine?" grinned Hawley. "Corbett — the one that busted out of the territorial pen a little while back? I got a hunch he's right here — I mean here in this hotel. That was Red Durkin with the jasper in the fancy suit. Red busted out with Steve Corbett."

"I don't want to get involved with a bunch of jailbirds," protested Millane.

"Stay quiet, leave all the talkin' to me," advised Hawley, "and maybe we won't have to fret about English Eddie. Maybe Corbett and his boys'll take that chore off our hands — and no charge. So how d'you like *that*? We sit back, let *them* handle the dirty work. Neat, huh?"

"You aren't making sense," complained the gambler.

Grinning complacently, Hawley ambled up to the desk.

"Red-haired gent looks like a feller I used to know. Cattlebuyer, right?"

"Why, yes," nodded the clerk. "Mister Dangar from Chicago."

The least I could do is stop by and say howdy," drawled Hawley. "What's his room number?"

"Number Twelve," the clerk told him. "Ground floor rear." He gestured to the alcove. "I wonder if you could persuade him to stay."

"No chance," shrugged Hawley. "When Dangar decides to go — he always goes."

Tagged by the apprehensive Millane, he sauntered along the ground floor passage and rapped at the door numbered 12. After a moment, the key rattled in the lock. The door opened just two inches, and Millane glimpsed portion of the redhead's face, also a leveled pistol.

"Easy, Red," whispered Hawley. "Remember me, don't you? Steve in there?"

"I'll be damned . . ." began Durkin. He muttered something over his shoulder, answering a barely audible question. Then, opening the door wider, he subjected Millane to a searching scrutiny. "Who's he?"

"He's with me," muttered Hawley. "You don't have to worry about him. Listen, Red, I know somethin' Steve ought to know."

Obeying Durkin's gesture, he moved into the room with Millane. Durkin closed and locked the door, while Hawley traded greets with the handsomely-tailored, thickset man stowing bundles of banknotes into a valise. The window was down and the shade drawn. The door opening into the next room was open, and Avery and another man lounged there, puffing on cigars and returning Millane's wary appraisal.

"Like old times huh Steve?" grinned

Hawley. "You always worked with three sidekicks. Four's plenty for any job, you used to say."

Corbett finished packing the cash and stood up, his broad, clean-shaven face devoid of expression.

"Good to see you, Brett," he nodded "Who's your tinhorn friend?"

"Name of Millane — from Omaha," offered Hawley. "Like I told Red, you don't have to worry about him."

"That's Jesse Willet," said Corbett, gesturing to the man standing beside Avery. "We busted out together, Red and me, and Jesse was our outside contact. The other jasper is Cole Avery — joined us a couple weeks back. Mighty useful feller is Cole."

"Got an answer for every problem," bragged Avery, grinning at Millane. "That's what they say about me."

"I should've guessed it was you pulled this bank job, Steve," drawled Hawley, helping himself to a chair. "The kind of job you were braggin' about. Remember? Back in the big pen,

227

just before they turned me loose?"

"I could afford to brag to you, Brett," grinned Corbett. "Knew you'd keep your mouth shut."

"The fire was the clincher," said Hawley. "You were countin' on a mess of smoke — a lot of citizens runnin' round in circles."

"I wasn't counting on that hullabaloo in Main Street," said Corbett. "Couldn't have happened at a better time."

"Just perfect for us," remarked Willet.

"All you had to do," guessed Hawley, "was climb through that window and hustle around front . . . "

"We were rigged in dusters and Stetsons — bandanas over our faces," Corbett said calmly. "No chance the banker could describe us. It went well, Brett. Except I had to knife some fool that tried to get in my way."

"Then you got out by way of the rear door and set fire to the old warehouse," said Hawley.

"The fire served a double purpose,

old buddy," grinned Corbett. "We had to get rid of our disguises. I mean *really* get rid of 'em."

"Nobody spotted you in the alley?" prodded Hawley.

"We had Cole standing guard," muttered Durkin. "Nobody spotted us. We just climbed back in here — and that was that."

"Some sharp operator, ain't he?" Hawley challenged Millane, nodding to Corbett. "In the big pen, Steve used to say as how he was through with tryin' to outrun a posse. Next time he hit a bank, he'd hide close by — the last place the law'd look for him."

"It'll work just fine," said Corbett. "We arrived by stage. We leave the same way. Eleven o'clock tomorrow. Red and me, we're supposed to be buyers for a Chicago meat-packing outfit. Cole and Jesse are fronting for a tent show. They even had posters printed!"

"I know," nodded Hawley. "I saw 'em."

"Listen, even if there *was* an Overton Repertory, I wouldn't expect 'em to play in a burg as dangerous as this," declared Avery, winking at Millane.

"I congratulate you gents," Millane said quietly. "Especially you, Corbett. Hawley called you a smart operator, and he sure wasn't fooling."

"Everything smooth," muttered Corbett. "No rough edges. No problems."

"You got *one* problem, old pal, and that's why I had to look you up," said Hawley. The other men traded frowns. Corbett lounged in a chair with his boots resting on the tightly-packed valise, his face expressionless. "Call it a favor, for old times sake. Friendly warnin', Steve."

"About . . . ?" challenged Corbett.

"You must've been followed, after you made your break," said Hawley.

"If some law-boy's been taggin' us, this'll be the first we knew of it," frowned Willet. "We covered our back-trail good."

"He's a Pinkerton — special agent'd

be my guess," offered Hawley. "Me and Gus saw him in Omaha. He was showin' your picture around, Steve."

"The hell he was," breathed Corbett.

"And now he's here — in Hortonville," declared Hawley.

"You sure?" gasped Durkin.

"Maybe he's damn near as smart as you, Steve," muttered Hawley. "Wait till you hear *this*. He makes believe he's English!"

"English?" prodded Corbett.

"Calls himself Roderick," said Hawley. "Even got himself a job."

Millane contributed a few words. Hawley's audacity had startled him, but, like a good poker-player, he rallied quickly.

"He's supposed to be a private tutor," he told Corbett.

"That was his pupil, the girl who started the riot."

"You try leavin' on tomorrow's eastbound, and the local badge-toters'll scarce notice," drawled Hawley. "But this Roderick, he's somethin' else. I'm bettin' he'll be watchin' the depot. And, if he recognizes you . . . "

"He's *bound* to recognize me," scowled Corbett. "A lousy Pinkerton . . . !" He swore bitterly. "Likely one of the same bunch that nailed me after the Pierce City job."

"I figured you ought to know," shrugged Hawley.

"Yeah, sure," nodded Corbett. "And I'm beholden , Brett."

"Steve, we'll have to take care of him," warned Durkin.

"You'd best come on up to our room," urged Hawley, rising from his chair. "He went into a store with the girl and her old man a little while ago. Could be they're still in there. From our window you'd see him easy."

"We'll need to know what he looks like," muttered Willet.

"Fetch a couple bottles," ordered Corbett, as he got to his feet. "We'll make it look like we're having a little party in Brett's room."

Some ten minutes later, when Little

Jake again moved out of the Bon Ton, the street was quiet. He darted wary glances to right and left, then muttered to his daughter and her escorts.

"I guess it's safe for her to show herself now."

Kate emerged, her gloved hand through Roderick's arm, the Texans following.

"Is Hortonville always so lively?" Roderick nervously enquired. "Great Scot! The way those men crowded about Miss Kate . . . "

"That's what I hankered to know," said Jake, grinning gleefully. "I craved to see what'd happen, when them bucks sighted Kate in her new finery."

"Should we stay?" wondered Roderick. "I mean — is it safe to risk a repetition?"

"A what?" frowned Jake.

"What Ed means," explained Larry, "is maybe it'll happen again."

"We'll stay for supper," Jake decided. "I want Kate should be waited on like a lady of quality by them pussy-footin' jaspers in the white jackets at the Ravello hashhouse." He chuckled in anticipation. "To eat at Ravello's, Mayor Kelso and his wife gets rigged up like Christmas trees. All the other high-toned females too. Well, by golly, ain't none of 'em gonna shine as bright as my Kate this night!"

"Where to now?" demanded Larry.

"First we'll kinda promenade a ways," grinned Jake. "Then we'll pay a few sociable visits. Preacher Hancock and his wife and sister. And, come to think of it, we could look in at the Puckeridge place. Horrie's laid up with a busted head, got clobbered by them bank bandits. Only nachral old friends'd come pay their respects, right? And that wife of his, that Zena Puckeridge, I swear she's so damn high-falutin' — acts like she was blood-kin to the last three presidents of this here U.S.A. I want to see *her* face when she looks Kate over. C'mon, let's walk." As they began moving along the sidewalk, he glared over his shoulder at the

Texans. "You can tag us — but keep your doggone distance."

Unoffended by this curt rebuff, well and truly accustomed to Jake's ways, the drifters grinned blandly.

"Sure, old timer," nodded Stretch. "Don't you fret. We won't shame you."

They sauntered toward the corner of Main and Garfield, the tree-lined street on which the homes of Hortonville's wealthier citizens were located. From the window of the room shared by Hawley and Millane, Steve Corbett and his cronies stared intently at the handsome Englishman on Kate Jarvis's left side.

"That's him, huh?" frowned Corbett.

"He's the one," nodded Hawley. "And mind what I told you, Steve. You can't take a chance on him catchin' sight of you."

"As if you need to remind me," scowled Corbett.

"You ready for a suggestion, Steve?" prodded Avery. "Remember me? I got an answer for everything."

"Well?" challenged Corbett.

"I guarantee this Pinkerton never saw *me* before," drawled Avery. "You and Red sure, but not me. So I'm the one ought to take care of him."

"That sheriff and his deputy, they're apt to get curious, if Roderick ends up in an alley with a knife in his back," warned Durkin. "Or a bullet-wound. Or his head stove in. And, next thing you know, they'll be checkin' on every stranger in town."

"I already thought of that," grinned Avery. "So — no rough stuff. Just leave it to me."

"I want to know how you plan on handling it," insisted Corbett.

"It won't be a bullet nor a knife," Avery assured him. "It'll be bellyache. The fatal kind."

"You'll — poison him?" frowned Millane.

"Nothing to it," chuckled Avery. "Sleight of hand, boys. Thirsty weather for the time of year, right? Mister Roderick buys himself a beer, maybe a shot of whiskey or a cup of coffee. And I'll be close. Close enough to spike his drink."

"How would you get the stiff?" Corbett demanded. "You can't just buy it from a druggist."

"Hell, no," shrugged Avery. "So I visit a doctor." He coughed and patted his chest, grinning and winking. "Been meaning to get something for this cough ever since we hit this burg."

"You'll steal what you need," guessed Hawley.

"Mighty slick he is," drawled Willet. "He could steal your belt and you wouldn't know it till your pants fell down."

"Better get started, Cole," frowned Corbett. "It might take longer than you think."

"Be seeing you," said Avery.

He sketched them a cheery salute and hurried away and, when the door closed after him, Corbett voiced a remark that caused Millane's scalp to crawl.

"If Avery fumbles it and gets himself arrested, we'll have to shut his mouth." Noting Millane's reaction, he grinned at Hawley and observed, "Your friend is squeamish."

"This Avery, you're thinkin' he might talk?" challenged Hawley.

"Like he always claims, he's got an answer for everything," muttered Corbett. "He works good, Brett. Until the chips are down. And then he's apt to lose his nerve."

"I've noticed," grunted Durkin. "Well, what the hell? If he gets rid of the Pinkerton and stays out of trouble, he'll collect his share of that bank loot. Otherwise — there'll be a bigger share for the rest of us."

Within the hour, Cole Avery had acquired a small bottle with a label showing the death's-head symbol. Linus McGowan, the elder of Hortonville's resident physicians, examined the fast-talking stranger for imaginary bronchial and stomach conditions and dismissed him as a hypochondriac, never suspecting that his medicine closet had been tampered with while his back was turned.

But it wasn't until 6.45 that evening that Avery saw his chance to dispose of Edward Roderick. The two posses had returned to town after a fruitless search of the surrounding terrain. At the Western Union office, Deputy Bloomfeld was wiring Omaha, North Loup and several towns south and west of Horton County. In conference with Horrie Puckeridge at the banker's home, Sheriff Trager pondered every detail of the robbery and tried to reassure him. But Puckeridge was pessimistic.

"You'll never find them," he declared. "A mighty successful operation — from their point of view. The bank's safe emptied, a client butchered and Nathan Gilbey laid up with concussion. And they made a clean getaway, Amos. By the time the posses were moving out, they must have been well on their way to the county line. No use alerting the other law enforcement agencies. The thieves will rest a while in some isolated hideout, then divide their spoils and go their separate ways."

Closely followed by the man in the checked suit, Little Jake, his beautiful daughter and her handsome tutor entered the town's most exclusive restaurant. Larry and Stretch, willing to postpone their supper for the sake of keeping the Englishman under surveillance, loitered in the dark alley beside Ravello's, watching a waiter conduct the Double J people to a centre table. Jake made himself comfortable and, after noting the admiring glances aimed at Kate by the other diners, passed the menu to Roderick.

"You order for us, Ed." He was inclined to use Roderick's christian name nowadays, being more than satisfied with his handiwork. "We'll have somethin' real fancy — and expensive."

The side window was closed but, through the panes, the Texans had a clear view of the party. Stretch, yawning boredly, remarked,

"We tagged 'em all afternoon, and never nobody tried to get close enough to talk to Ed."

"But he didn't dream it," countered Larry. "Some galoot *did* warn him. So maybe he's still a target."

"And you still hanker to know why," nodded Stretch.

Avery, seated at the table nearest the Double J party, heard Roderick give their order. He kept his head down, pretending to study his menu, while a second waiter hovered over him.

"Coffee for the lady and Mister Jarvis, I think," finished Roderick. "And, for me, tea of course."

"Proves he's real English, huh Kate honey?" grinned Jake. "Never knew an Englishman didn't hanker for tea."

Avery gave his order and, as the waiter made to move away, delayed him with a question.

"Who's boss-cook of this place now?"

"Mister Leo Ravello," offered the waiter. "He's related to the owner."

"Like to pay my respects while he's fixing my steak," smiled Avery, rising from his chair. "I think we have a mutual friend, Mister Ravello and me."

Before the waiter could protest that diners weren't allowed in the kitchen, Avery had entered the chef's domain and was introducing himself, warmly shaking his hand and congratulating him on the restaurant's reputation, its elegant cuisine and its kitchen, the cleanest he had found outside of Omaha. Completely disarmed by this flattery, the chef insisted on giving him a guided tour and, during this diversion, Avery spotted the only teapot in sight. Obviously the Englishman was the only tea-drinker in the restaurant; every other diner had ordered coffee.

When Avery returned to his table, the tiny bottle was back in his vest pocket, but half-empty.

With their salivary glands working over time, the Texans watched Kate and her escorts dispose of their three courses, paying little attention to the jasper in the checked suit seated nearby. After the dessert, the waiter delivered coffee to Jake and his daughter and made a small ceremony of placing cup and saucer and teapot before Roderick, who thanked him with an affable nod.

"Miss Kate . . . " he began.

"Oh, sure, I remember," she smiled, reaching for the teapot. "Shall I pour, Mister Roderick?"

"If you please," said Roderick.

"Real ladylike," aproved Jake, "Got to hand it to you, Ed. You're sure earnin' your pay."

Within a moment of sipping his tea, the Englishman was slumping in his chair, his face contorted, and Jake was on his feet, bellowing for a doctor. While Stretch frowned perplexedly, Larry growled an oath and asserted,

"Some sonfabitch slipped him somethin' — and I reckon I know who!"

"What in tarnation . . . ?" began Stretch.

"I recall there was just one jasper visited the kitchen," muttered Larry, studying the man in the checked suit. "No way he could spike Ed's drink right there in the dining room. But maybe — in the kitchen . . . "

"Damn and blast!" breathed Stretch.

"You help get Ed to the doctor — and fast," ordered Larry. "I'm gonna follow that sneakin' polecat and . . . "

"Meanin' the galoot in the checkered suit," guessed Stretch. "Why, sure. He went out back just before . . . "

"Time enough later for talk," growled Larry. "Get movin'."

Avery was rising to leave, dropping a banknote beside his half-finished supper, when Stretch barged in and made his way to the excited group hovering about the stricken man. Gathering Roderick into his arms, he snapped commands at the confused Jake and his worried daughter.

"We're gettin' out of here — *now*. Lead me to the doc's house. Larry figures Ed's been poisoned. Only way we can save him is get him to a doc — muy pronto."

"Dudley house is closest," muttered Jake. "Let's go."

At the entrance, Avery stood aside to permit Jake and the girl to pass. They hurried out with Stretch following, carrying the Englishman, and then Avery sauntered to the sidewalk, lit a cigar and began strolling toward the McQuade House. He was grinning smugly, congratulating himself, until Larry's drawling challenge reached him.

"Hold it right there, mister! I want a word with you!"

Avery glanced over his shoulder and kept moving. Sweat gleamed on his suddenly flushed face; he was unnerved by the demeanor of the tall, roughly-garbed man striding toward him.

"I don't know you," he called. "Quit bothering me, or I'll have you arrested."

"If I'm wrong about you, I'll beg your doggone pardon," Larry coldly retorted.

"But — if you're the sonofabitch that poisoned Roderick — you're sure as hell gonna pay for it."

Avery's action was typical, and exactly what Steve Corbett had predicted. In panic, he emptied his shoulder-holster and cut loose. The bullet whined past Larry's head, as he drew his Colt and flopped to one knee. Avery fired again and again. A slug tore an inch from the brim of Larry's Stetson. Another kicked grit into his face, as he dropped flat and leveled his six-gun. He cocked and fired, aiming for Avery's legs, and then Avery's anguished yell was rising loud above the din of gunfire and he was reeling drunkenly, sprawling on his back.

Slowly, Larry rose to his feet. He was still gripping his smoking Colt, when the law arrived, Bloomfeld challenging him from the west sidewalk, Trager bounding toward him from the law office, hefting a shotgun.

"You won't need that cannon," Larry drawled, as the boss-lawman reached the dead man. "Won't be no more shootin' — 'less your deputy gets trigger-happy."

Undismayed by the proxmity of Bloomfeld's leveled gun, he ejected his spent shell, tugged a fresh one from his belt and reloaded. He knew he wouldn't be seeing the inside of a cell this night. There had been witnesses. A dozen or more locals were moving off the sidewalks, converging on Trager and the body sprawled in the dust.

8

Greed, Guilt and Guns

WHILE bitterly resenting Larry's cold calm, Sheriff Trager was forced to heed the many witnesses, all of them insisting Avery had fired three shots at Larry before he retaliated.

"You got questions to answer just the same," the lawman warned Larry.

"Ask away," shrugged Larry.

"Not here," growled Trager. "We'll talk at the funeral parlor, while my deputy checks this jasper's pockets."

The curious locals were dismissed and the body carried to the premises of an undertaker. There, while Bloomfeld turned out the dead man's pockets with the undertaker standing by, Trager studied the Texan intently and put his first question.

"Why'd you brace him anyway? One of those witnesses claims you accused him of somethin'. Exactly what?"

"I got a shrewd hunch he poisoned a friend of mine at the Ravello restaurant," drawled Larry, as he rolled a cigarette. "Can't claim I was dead sure — until he lost his head and pulled a gun on me."

Bloomfeld held up the tiny bottle with the death's head label, traded frowns with his boss and muttered,

"Some kind of poison. Bet your badge on it."

"By now, Ed Rockerick's gettin' doctored," opined Larry, "I don't know if any doc can save him. Guess it depends how much of that stuff he drank, and how soon the doc got to work on him." He went on to tell of his vigil at the restaurant's side window and followed that with an account of the ambush of the Double J party en route from Omaha to Horton County. "What it adds up to," he explained, "is somebody wants this Roderick six feet underground. But don't ask me why." He shrugged nonchalantly and lit his cigarette. "I planned on scarin' some answers out of this jasper."

"With your bullet in his heart, he couldn't answer any questions," frowned the deputy. "Why didn't you try creasin' him?"

"I'm a lousy shot," lied Larry, pensively eyeing the mortal wound. "Guess it was too dark for me to draw a clear bead."

"Yeah, well, with him triggerin' wild at you, I guess you can't be blamed for defendin' yourself," Trager said grudgingly. "All right, Olaf, how about identification?"

"Couple hundred in his wallet," Bloomfeld reported. "Letter of introduction calls him . . . " he squinted at the name, "Cole Avery — representing the Overton Theatrical Enterprises. Oh, sure, I remember him now. Him and some other feller been puttin' up those posters all over town."

"So we know his name and the outfit

he was workin' for — and we know he poisoned Roderick," mused Trager.

"Roderick bein' that dude hired by Little Jake," offered Bloomfeld. "The English feller. Private teacher for Kate."

"What we don't know" complained Trager, "is *why'd* he do it?"

"Maybe this gent can explain," suggested Bloomfeld, his gaze on the man moving in from the undertaker's office.

Jesse Willet nodded respectfully to the lawmen, advanced to the table and stared sadly at the dead man's ashen face.

"I couldn't believe it, gents," he muttered. Corbett had rehearsed him well. "When I heard Avery had been shot in a street-fight, I just couldn't believe . . . "

"You two were workin' for the same outfit," prodded Trager.

"The Overton company, yes," nodded Willet. "But I can't say I knew him very well. They hired him only a month ago. Seemed a friendly, harmless kind of feller."

"Ever hear him mention a man named Roderick?" demanded Trager.

"Roderick?" Willet wrinkled his brow and stroked his nose. "Why, no. The name is new to me. Don't believe I ever heard it."

"Nothin' else you can tell us about Avery?" challenged Trager.

"Nothing," said Willet. "I'm sorry."

"All right, you can go," said Trager. "But I might want to talk to you again later, Mister . . . ?"

"Willet. Jesse Willet. I'm at the McQuade House, but I was planning on leaving tomorrow. The eleven o'clock stage."

"If I need you, I'll look you up before then," promised Trager. He watched Willet walk out, then remarked to his deputy, "I guess I should check on Roderick now, find out if he's still alive."

"My guess is the doc'll feed him an emetic," offered the undertaker.

"Something to make him bring up."

"Would that be enough to save his life?" wondered Trager.

"Depends," shrugged the undertaker. "You'd best take that little bottle with you, so the doc can identify the poison. Maybe this Roderick'll live. There are all kinds of poison, Amos. Some act faster than others. I'm no expert. You'll have to ask the doc."

"Even if Roderick's strong enough to talk, you'll get nothin' from him," drawled Larry.

"Somebody wants him dead — and he doesn't know why?" frowned Bloomfeld.

"I already asked him," shrugged Larry. "He claims he just don't know. And I believe him."

"Olaf, you and me best get back to the office," Trager decided. "Could be we got a bulletin on this jasper. Maybe Avery wasn't his real name."

"Take us hours to check all our files," sighed Bloomfeld.

"I know it," nodded Trager. "But we

can't leave it like this. Got to follow up on it." As they followed Larry out, it suddenly occured to him that he hadn't asked the Texan's name. "All I know is you're one of Little Jake's new hands. What're you called?"

"Lawrence," said Larry.

"All right, Lawrence, we only have two doctors in this town," said Trager. "Old Linus McGowan and Cliff Dudley."

"I'll check 'em both," nodded Larry.

"Ask the doc to let me know about Roderick," said Trager.

"Uh huh, I'll do that," Larry promised.

When they reached the main stem, Trager directed him to the homes of Doctors Dudley and McGowans. Because the Dudley home was closest, he headed in that direction. A familiar, gangling figure paced the sidewalk near the front gate, and he knew he would search no further. Stretch greeted him with a preoccupied nod and remarked,

"Next time some galoot tries to kill

me, I hope he don't use poison."

"How about Ed?" asked Larry.

"He's gonna be okay. But — Holy Hannah — if you could've seen how that sawbones handled him . . . "

Three factors had combined to save the Englishman's life on this occasion — the fact that he was delivered to the Dudley home in double-quick time, the fact that the medico was at home when they arrived, and the most important fact of all — Roderick's prompt and violent reaction to the emetic.

"I never saw a man so all-fired sick in all my born days," Stretch declared. "But the doc claims that's what saved him."

"Where's Ed now?" Larry demanded.

"They put him to bed," said Stretch. "The doc says he'll be strong enough to travel back to the spread tomorrow, most likely. But not tonight. Tonight he has to rest. Shock to the system, the doc says."

"You know which room he's in?" frowned Larry, glancing at the house.

"Uh huh," grunted Stretch. "Why?"

"Go hide yourself and keep an eye on the window," ordered Larry. "I'll find you in a little while."

"You thinkin' — they'll try again?"

"They just might, if they hear he's still alive. You stake out now, while I talk to the sawbones. How about Kate and the old man?"

"About ready to leave, I guess."

"Bueno. Get goin'."

Stretch loafed away toward the side of the house, while Larry moved up the walk to the front door, reaching the porch just as Kate and her father emerged. With them was Cliff Dudley, a rotund, ruddy-complexioned healer who surveyed Larry through steel-rimmed spectacles. Kate performed introductions, after which Larry told the rancher.

"We'll be stayin' overnight. When Ed's fit to travel home, he can ride double with me, or maybe we'll rent a rig."

For once, Little Jake was subdued,

resisting the urge to rage and rant.

"He sure got hisself an enemy, and no mistake," he mumbled.

"One *less* enemy," said Larry. "I tagged the galoot that slipped him the poison." Offering the tiny bottle to Dudley, he explained, "The deputy took this from his pocket."

"Caught up with the killer, did you?" prodded Jake.

"Caught up with him," nodded Larry. "but I still don't know why he did it, Jake. There was a shootout."

"He's — dead?" frowned Kate.

"And then some," shrugged Larry. The medico grimaced impatiently and began retreating into the house.

"If you folks'll excuse me, ought to be checking this stuff," he explained. "When I've identified it, I'll know if the patient will need further treatment."

"We're obliged, Doc," muttered Jake. He was silent for a long moment after Dudley had closed the door. "All right, I'll take Kate home now, and you bucks stay close — 'case Ed needs your help."

As he took his daughter's arm, he squinted pensively and confided, "I got to likin' that dude, and not just on account of all he's done for Kate. Don't care what kind of panhandler he is. We made a bargain, and he stuck to his end of it, and I admire a man that holds to his word."

Larry escorted them to the front gate, watched them move away toward the main street, then ambled around the south side of the house. Through the window of Dudley's surgery he saw the medico checking the contents of a cabinet. Moving around back, he made for the north corner. Stretch whistled softly and he ambled onward, having marked his partner's stakeout. In the bushes a few yards from an open window, they hunkered side by side for a muttered parley.

"Dunno if Ed's sleepin' yet, but that's where he's at," offered Stretch. "Doc said he needs plenty air. That's why the window's open."

"Okay," nodded Larry. "Kate and

the old man're headed home. The galoot that spiked the teapot ended up with a slug in his heart, so we won't learn anything from him. But I'm bettin' he wasn't the only one."

"I heard shootin'," said Stretch. "That was you and him, huh?"

"Me, him, and some other hombre," muttered Larry. "I aimed for his left leg. Figured to knock him off his feet. He spun just as I triggered — and the reason he spun was that slug in his heart."

"Hey now!" breathed Stretch.

"This Trager ain't the smartest sheriff I ever knew," drawled Larry. "He's satisfied I killed that poisoner in self-defense. I didn't argue about it, because I don't hanker to waste time."

"More'n one of 'em," guessed Stretch. "They were afeared the poisoner'd talk, so they couldn't let you take him alive."

"That's how it looks to me," said Larry. He felt at his vest pockets, eager for another smoke, but deciding against it. The glow of a cigarette could alert anybody creeping to that open window. "No more talk now. From now on, we wait."

"Might wait the whole damned night," frowned Stretch.

"But their vigil ended some 45 minutes later. They filled their hands and, along the level barrels of their Colts, followed the furtive movements of the man sidling along the near wall of the house. Reaching a window, he scratched a match and pressed his face to the panes. Beyond was the Dudleys' ground floor parlor, empty. He edged along to the open window of the room where the Englishman slept, lit another match, peered inside, then threw a leg over the sill.

By the time Russ Webb had found and lit a lamp, the Texans were crouched by the window. Had he drawn a knife or any other weapon, his life would have ended then and there. But, to their surprise, he squatted on the edge of the bed and began slapping Roderick's cheeks, rousing him. Roderick came awake, groggy from the sedative given him by the medico.

"Doctor Dudley . . . ?" He yawned and began raising himself. "What now . . . ?"

"It's me again," growled Webb. "And now I guess you believe me, huh Roderick? Now you know I wasn't lyin'. They damn near finished you tonight, didn't they? I heard all about it."

"Well, well, well." The Englishman grinned wearily. "My nocturnal visitor reappears. Still afflicted by toothache, I see."

"Don't joke, Roderick," chided Webb. He felt at his bandana to make sure it hadn't slipped. "You can't afford to refuse me. I guess you realize that at last. Them killers gonna try again, nothin' surer. No way you can save your hide — 'less I tell you who they are. And you know my price."

"One thousand dollars," nodded

Roderick. "Very reasonable, I'm sure, but you might as well demand *ten* thousand. I've no way of . . ."

"Get it, damn you!" snapped Webb. "Borrow it — or *steal* it! I won't wait — and neither will them killers!"

"I presume it would be useless my appealing to your sense of justice," sighed Roderick. "Whatever information you have should be conveyed to the law authorities."

"You pay my price," Webb retorted, "or I tell nobody nothin'."

"Nobody's payin' you nothin'," growled Stretch. "But you're gonna tell us plenty, boy. You're gonna tell us *everything*."

Webb leapt to his feet, his right hand flashing to his holster, then freezing on his gunbutt. The sharp clicking sound of the Texans cocking their Colts was ample discouragement at such deadly short range.

"Lift 'em," ordered Larry. Webb's hands shot up. "Now step clear of the bed." He climbed into the room.

Stretch followed, nodding affably to the perplexed Roderick. "Take his iron — and let's see his face."

Relieved of his pistol and his bandana mask, the intruder blinked apprehensively at the Texans. Larry seized a fistful of his shirtfront, glared into his face and brandished his Colt. While he snarled threats, Stretch pleaded with him. It was an old ruse, one they had used many times, but it succeeded; Webb was completely intimidated.

"He wouldn't have told Ed a thing!" Larry accused. "He'd have taken his money — and let those killers finish what they started!"

"No . . . " gasped Webb.

"So — the hell with him!" raged Larry. "Why don't I dent his lousy head, throw him across a horse and take him to the river?"

"You wouldn't do *that* again?" Stretch recoiled in horror. "Last time you gunwhipped a feller — it was that cardsharp in Utah. You tied him to a rock and shoved him into the San

Juan — and all I could see was the bubbles — and it made me sick to my stomach!"

"It's all he deserves!" insisted Larry.

"I wasn't gonna hold out!" groaned Webb. "Listen — I'll tell you everything — and it won't cost him a dime!"

"Don't hit him, runt," pleaded Stretch.

"Just a couple times," scowled Larry. "I crave to see him bleed."

"I *say*!" gasped Roderick.

"You butt outa this, Panhandler!" snapped Larry.

"He's no panhandler!" Webb said quickly. "He's rich! His old man died — and he inherits! There was — a letter for him. Only — they read it — and . . . !"

"My father — dead . . . ?" challenged Roderick.

"There was this letter," mumbled Webb. As Larry let go of him, he retreated to a chair and began mopping at his face. "I was listenin' outside her window, when they talked to Brett."

"Brett Hawley," sighed Webb, "Him and the tinhorn, they plan on killin' Roderick, so she'll be a rich widow."

"Is he speaking of — Melva?" prodded Roderick.

"Take it easy, Ed," advised Stretch. "You oughn't be gettin' excited."

"A little late for you to think of *that*, isn't it?" The Englishman was trembling in agitation. "If what he says is the truth . . ."

"It better be," growled Larry. "Go on, snooper. Tell it all. I want to know everything you heard."

In defeat, Webb saw only one hope for survival. He recounted the gist of all he had heard while eavesdropping outside Melva Roderick's window, admitted to taking part in the ambush of the Double J party and described Hawley as a desperado with an eye to the main chance. Millane, he assured the Texans, was just as treacherous.

"And my wife — the beautiful Melva — is the most treacherous of the three," muttered Roderick. "The female of the species — deadlier than the male."

"Ed, we're sorry about your old man," frowned Stretch.

"But we ain't apologizin' for callin' you a deadbeat," declared Larry.

"Heaven knows you owe me no apologies." The Englishman shrugged sadly. "It seems I'm still indebted to you — for my life." He bowed his head and brooded a moment. "I wish you could have known Sir Nigel, my illustrious sire. A gentleman to the core. A true aristocrat. I could never hope to take his place . . ."

"But I guess you'll have to try," said Larry.

"Yes, you're right of course." Roderick eyed him steadily. "I must return to the old country, claim my inheritance . . ."

"You're the lucky one, mister," mumbled Webb. "You'll live rich and easy the rest of your days — on account of the old man made a new will. He left you the whole shebang."

"And, if Melva had her way, *she'd* inherit," said Roderick, "as my widow."

"And Millane and Hawley'd be cut in," growled Larry.

"I'll divorce her of course," said Roderick. "Yes — first thing in the morning — I'll wire the Omaha law authorities. And then I must arrange my passage home. No. Come to think of it, no point in my leaving the country until my affairs are finalized. The divorce — my obligation to Mister Jarvis . . ."

"Not so doggone fast," chided Larry. "You're forgettin' somethin'."

"Somethin' real important, Sir Ed," drawled Stretch. "Such as it still ain't safe for you to show your face. This Hawley jasper and the tinhorn, they ain't about to quit." He frowned at Webb and raised another question. "How about the galoot that poisoned Ed? If he wasn't Hawley nor Millane . . ."

"I dunno about him — and that's the truth," said Webb. "I guess — Hawley

267

or Millane must've hired him for the job."

"That makes it just a mite more interestin'," Larry said thoughtfully.

"What do you mean?" asked Roderick.

"I mean how many jaspers are tryin' to kill you," drawled Larry.

"Great Scot!" frowned Roderick.

"I beat 'em to Horton County," offered Webb. "They ain't been here more'n a couple days."

"You're suggesting they may have — hired an entire band of assassins — to dispose of me?" The Englishman grimaced impatiently. "See here, Larry old chap, that hardly seems likely."

"Maybe not, but one thing's for sure," opined Larry. "The jasper that poisoned you was tied in with Hawley and Millane."

"So where do we stand now?" demanded Stretch. "We got a couple names — Hawley and Millane — and we've found out why they want him dead. But we don't know what they look like."

"*He* does," countered Larry, jerking a thumb at Webb. "And he's gonna show us."

"Hell, no!" wailed Webb. "If Brett spotted me with you two, he'd shoot and run!"

The Texans swung their guns toward the door. Doc Dudley had knocked, and now the door was opening. He thrust his head into the room, frowned reproachfully and asked what seemed a fair question.

"What the devil's happening here? My patient is under sedation. Mister Roderick — damnitall — who are these men?"

Larry holstered his Colt, drew the medico into the room and offered him a terse explanation. At first bewildered, Dudley disciplined himself, hanging on Larry's every word until the unlikely story began making sense. He trudged to the bed, checked his patient's pulse and heartbeat and commented,

"Considering his close call from death by poisioning — and the news of inheriting a title and a fortune — he's in fairly good shape."

"But still in danger," Larry pointed out.

"Obviously," agreed Dudley. "Until the killers are apprehended. So what would you have me do? Send for the sheriff?"

"If we drop this in Trager's lap, he'll start a search and make a lot of noise," opined Larry. "You know what that means? It could mean Hawley and Millane will be warned off."

"They make a run for it, maybe get clear away," said Stretch, "and we're back where we started."

"I'm willing to co-operate," offered Dudley. He added, carefully, "Anything within reason."

"What d'you say, runt?" prodded Stretch.

"I say we sit tight till mornin'," drawled Larry. "We wait, and you can bet that's what *they're* doin'. Waitin'."

"To find out if Ed's gonna live or die," guessed Stretch.

"Around mid-mornin', Doc'll tell the townsfolk it's all over," said Larry. "He did his best, but Ed died anyway. And, sure as shootin', that news'll reach Hawley and Millane. They'll come out from wherever they're hidin' and head for Omaha. At least they'll try."

"And that's when we nail 'em." Stretch nodded approvingly. "Yeah, I like that fine. We settle their hash — just when they think they've won."

"This would be — downright unethical," protested Dudley. "I'm sure my patient will be fully recovered by morning, yet you ask me . . ."

"We're askin'," nodded Larry. "You know *why* we're askin'. So what d'you say?"

"So . . ." Dudley shrugged helplessly. "So I'll do it."

"We'll bunk right here tonight, sleep on the floor," Larry told him. "When we move out tomorrow, we'll take this jasper with us." He nodded to Webb. "And there's just one more thing you can do for us, Doc. He needs some kind of disguise."

"We need for him to be with us," Stretch explained, "so he can identify Hawley and Millane. But we'd as soon keep him alive." He thought to ask Larry, "*What* kind of disguise?"

"Doc, how big is your wife?" frowned Larry.

"Generously proportioned is the term I'd use," said Dudley, glancing at Webb. "Maybe not as tall as this man, but certainly as broad."

"Hold on now . . . !" began Webb.

"Think Mrs Dudley'd oblige?" prodded Larry. "And keep her mouth shut?"

"She'd be delighted." The medico glanced at Webb again and chuckled softly. "Why, yes. I know she'd see the funny side of it."

In vain, Webb mumbled protests. He was silenced by his own bandana; Stretch gagged him with it before securing his wrists with his pants-belt and dumping him in a corner. The doctor left them then and, after some

90 minutes of brooding on his changed situation, Roderick closed his eyes. The Englishman was reflecting, just before sleep claimed him, that it was all too confused to be true. In the morning, he would awaken as the same English Eddie so well known in Omaha, a deadbeat with no future. His austere sire had seemed indestructible; it was still too much to believe Sir Nigel had gone to join his distinguished ancestors, and that he, the least worthy member of that noble family, had become Sir Edward Roderick, Baronet.

He awoke clear-headed and bedeviled by hunger, blinked against the bright sunlight streaming through the window and mumbled a question.

"What time is it?"

"With your belly empty, you sure sleep good," grinned Stretch.

"Ten o'clock," offered Larry.

Roderick propped himself up on his elbows and filled his eyes with the scene enacted in what had become a crowded spare bedroom. The Texans were

273

standing by, impatient to be out and about. Webb was suffering extremes of humiliation, and not without reason. Doc Dudley's bulky spouse had just finished rigging him in one of her gowns, and now the ensemble was complete. His feet bulged in her lace-up boots, the hem of the gown reached to his calves. He held a reticle and a parasol, his clean-shaven face red with embarrassment, as Liza Dudley secured a poke bonnet to his head.

"That ought to do it," she cheerfully remarked to her husband. "Just one thing though, Cliff. If my blue gingham gets shot full of holes, who's going to replace it?"

"Aw, hell," groaned Webb.

"Rest assured, madam, I'll make full restitution," muttered Roderick. He winced and dropped a hand to his stomach. "Doctor, I hate to impose, but I have such an appetite . . . !"

"Good sign," approved Dudley. "Liza, if you're through making Mister Webb beautiful . . . "

"That ain't funny," scowled Webb.

"Our patient could use some food," said the medico. "Start him on a bowl of broth, then get him onto solids." As his wife hurried out, he grinned reassuringly at the Texans. "All right, gentlemen, I did as you asked. Broke the sad news just twenty minutes ago."

"Twenty minutes," nodded Larry. "Bueno. Townfolks'll talk it around and, pretty soon, it'll get to Hawley and Millane."

"Time for us to take a little walk along Main," opined the taller Texan.

"I don't like this — not one little bit," fretted Webb.

"You do like I said," ordered Larry. "Point 'em out when you sight 'em, then go hide."

"But don't try to make a run for it," warned Stretch. "You'd look powerful strange — tryin' to straddle a horse in that get-up."

"You promised to protect me," Webb reminded them.

"We'll do our damnedest," muttered Larry. "But you'd better do right by us. Don't pull no fool tricks — such as pointin' us at the wrong men. We want Hawley and Millane, understand?" He nodded to Stretch to open the door. "Let's get started."

It was 10.25 when the disguised Russ Webb escorted by the Texans turned out of the side street and began moving along Main. In the lobby of the McQuade House, Corbett was being farewelled by Hawley and Millane, who had paid their bill and were ready to begin their return to Omaha. Durkin and Willet stood by the entrance, frowning impatiently toward the stage depot. With the desk-clerk well and truly out of earshot, Corbett traded grins with Hawley and remarked,

"This is the only way, Brett. The neat, clean way to take a bank."

"No sweat, huh pal?" chuckled Hawley. "You just climb on that eastbound stage — and that's an end of it."

"Leaving one of your sidekicks to be buried here in Hortonville," frowned Millane.

"Like Cole always said, he had an answer for everything," drawled Corbett. "Even pulled a gun and went trigger-happy, made it that much easier for me to shut his mouth, and nobody the wiser."

"You were damn lucky, Corbett," said Millane. "If you hadn't been watching from that alley . . ."

"Not luck, tinhorn," said Corbett. "Good management. I wasn't taking a chance Cole would bungle the job. When he came out of that restaurant and was challenged, I knew he'd panic — and he sure as hell did." He chuckled complacently. "We're clear now. The Pinkerton's too dead to bother us — so we're on our way."

"Us too," said Hawley. "We'll see you out, then head uptown and fetch our horses."

Corbett picked up the bulging valise, signaled his cronies and made for the entrance. The three bank-robbers quit the hotel and began sauntering toward the stagecoach depot, while Hawley and Millane descended the steps and made for the uptown stable where their horses awaited them.

"By yourself, you couldn't have pulled it off," Hawley jeered at the gambler.

"I'd have managed," shrugged Millane. "But I have to admit you're a fast-thinker, Hawley. That was quite a maneuver, lying to Corbett, convincing him Roderick was a Pinkerton."

"Before we leave, we'll have to stop by the doc's house or the funeral parlor," drawled Hawley. "Wherever they took the body."

"You mean . . . ?"

"Little question of identification," said Hawley. "The law has to know who he was. The newspapers too. That double-crossin' whore back in Omaha . . . "

"Don't call her that," protested Millane.

"She needs to prove she's a widow," Hawley pointed out, "and that he was the same Ed Roderick."

"So we identify the body," frowned Millane.

"And then you can wire Melva the good news," grinned Hawley.

They advanced three more paces and came to an abrupt halt. From the opposite sidewalk, Webb had spotted them and gasped a warning; he was gathering his skirts and scuttling into the nearest doorway, when the Texans stepped off the sidewalk, Larry bellowing a challenge, Stretch called to the locals to clear the street.

"That's as far as you go!"

When Larry's command assailed their ears, Corbett's cronies jumped to the wrong conclusion. Durkin whirled, spotted Deputy Bloomfeld emerging from a nearby barbershop and was sure the command had been bellowed by him. To Bloomfeld's astonishment, one of three men he had never seen before pulled a gun and cut loose at him.

"No . . . !" yelled Corbett. "You proddy fool!"

Bloomfeld flopped to his knees, his left arm bloody and useless, his big right hand pawing for his Colt, while the locals scattered for cover. The stage was rolling into Main from its south end, and Corbett realized he had no hope of leaving Hortonville as a passenger; Durkin's impulsive action started him cursing wildly.

"Find horses!" he gasped. "We'll have to make a run for it!"

The deputy's Colt roared. He missed Durkin, but the bullet sped on to crease Willet, who loosed an anguished yell, reeled drunkenly and sprawled in the dust. Larry, hurrying across Main to intercept Hawley and the gambler, saw Bloomfeld's predicament and assumed the other men to be Hawley's accomplices. He growled a command to Stretch, who emptied both holsters and began bounding toward the wounded deputy.

"Lie flat, badge-toter!" he yelled.

"You — and you . . . !" He hurled a warning after Corbett and Durkin, "quit runnin' and get your hands up!"

Reaching the mouth of an alley, the fleeing bank-robbers turned with their guns blazing. The taller Texan leapt and, like a gigantic grasshopper, flopped in front of Bloomfeld, shielding him with his body, then rolling over and lining his Colts on the desperadoes.

Larry, meanwhile, had almost reached the east sidewalk and the end of his violent career. In panic, Millane had drawn and fired at him, and that hastily-triggered slug missed Larry's head with only inches to spare. Recognizing Larry as one of the sharpshooters who had fought off his ambush, Hawley snarled a curse, jerked his Colt and sidled to cover, flopping behind a water-trough and leaving Millane to fend for himself. Millane re-cocked, took aim again, but was given no time for a second shot. Larry fired while throwing himself flat. His bullet slammed into the gambler's right shoulder and sent him lurching off the sidewalk to collapse in the street.

"You — behind the trough!" called Larry. "Throw your gun out!" You try for a shot, and you're finished!"

"Who the hell are you anyway?" Hawley challenged, raising his voice against the din of gunfire from downtown. And what d'you think you got on me?"

"I've got Roderick — alive!" retorted Larry. "And a galoot name of Webb!"

"Roderick — alive . . . !" Millane groaned and groveled in the dust. "Damn you, Hawley! You were — so damn sure . . . !"

Hawley's fury got the better of him. He took a chance and paid for it, rising quickly to level his gun at the prone and waiting Larry. Larry squeezed trigger and saw his victim topple away from the trough with his chest bloody.

Scrambling to his feet, Larry bellowed to Stretch and began running toward him. In the alleymouth, Corbett crouched beside Durkin, who was pallid and trembling, incapable of triggering another shot. His gun lay in the dust, his right hand bled and the agony of his wound had started his senses reeling.

"Gonna have to leave you, Red," growled Corbett. "Too bad, old buddy, but I'm playing for high stakes."

Ignoring Durkin's frantic pleas, he hefted the valise and began retreating along the alley. Stretch hastily signaled Larry, who returned to the east sidewalk and made for the alleymouth at a hard run, reaching it in time to sight Corbett at its far end.

His yelled challenge won a violent response. Corbett turned quickly, his pistol belching fire and death. Buffeted by the bullet creasing his left shoulder, Larry stumbled a pace to his right, and that movement saved his life; Corbett's second slug would otherwise have struck him dead centre. He returned fire, nudging his right elbow into his hip to steady his gunhand, and Corbett jerked convulsively, let go of his gun and the valise and clasped both hands to his face. Like an unstrung puppet, he crumpled to the dust; he was dead when Larry reached him.

Larry was rolling a cigarette one-handed, when Bloomfeld and Stretch entered the alley with the sheriff in tow.

"If you'll quit hollerin' long enough to give me a light," he chided the confused Trager, "I'll be glad to answer your questions."

"This feller needs a doctor, Amos," mumbled Bloomfeld. "And — damn and blast . . . " He squatted cross-legged, wincing from the pain of his broken arm, "he ain't the only one."

"Runt, why'd these other jaspers buy in?" demanded Stretch.

"I — could be wrong," grunted Larry, as Trager gave him a light. "But I think — when I challenged Hawley and the tinhorn — this hombre and his sidekicks thought I was challengin' *them*."

"Maybe they thought it was *me* hollerin' at 'em," offered Bloomfeld.

"Maybe that's why — they drew down on me."

Trager's questions were coming thick and fast, when it occurred to the taller Texan to nudge Corbett's body aside and investigate the valise. The sheriff's voice choked off, as Stretch snapped the catches and raised the lid, remarking,

"Ain't that a purty sight — all that happy lettuce?"

"By damn!" breathed Bloomfeld. "Hey, Amos d'you suppose . . . ?"

"The bank loot?" Trager squatted beside the deputy and, with trembling hands, lit a cigar. "Could be, Olaf. Could be."

"Hombre at the other end of the alley," drawled Stretch. "He's some toilworn, but alive. You get workin' on him and he'll likely tell you all you want to know. Meantime, I got to take my sidekick to the Dudley place. He needs patchin'."

"When Doc Dudley gets through, have him come to the jailhouse," begged Trager. He shook his head dazedly. "Two men shot dead — and three wounded. What a day!"

By early afternoon, when Roderick and the Texans headed back to Double J in a rented buggy, Sheriff Trager had his answers and several prisoners. Durkin, crazed with pain, had named Corbett as the murderer of Tom Gates and Cole Avery, and Trager had checked his files and established that Durkin was a survivor of the breakout from the territorial pen. Millane also would be held for trial on a charge of conspiracy to murder, thanks to the statement sworn to and signed by Russ Webb. Full details had been wired to the Omaha authorities.

"I'm glad I'll not be there, when Melva is taken into custody," Roderick confided to the Texans. "How much disgust and disappointment can one man cope with? I'll begin divorce proceedings upon my return to Omaha."

"Figure on travelin' as soon as you've rested up, huh?" prodded Stretch.

"Not quite that soon." The Englishman smiled wryly. "I believe I can afford to wait for the return of Mister Mitchell Firestone. The fact is — I'd hate to miss seeing the results of my labors, you know?"

"You want to be there," guessed Larry, "when Firestone's son gets an eyeful of Kate — rigged and talkin' like a lady."

"One should honor one's obligations," said Roderick. "Mister Jarvis and I have an agreement. Moreover, gentlemen, I have learned to admire and respect Miss Kate, a young lady who deserves to be happy. Obviously her best chance of happiness would be in marriage — to the man she loves."

★ ★ ★

Little Jake's cup was filled to overflowing on the day Mitch Firestone returned to Horton County. The young man's parents and a formidable deputation of Hammerhead riders were on hand to welcome him, when he descended from the stagecoach at the Hortonville depot, handsome, well-groomed and poised — until his gaze fastened on the fashionably-gowned beauty seated beside Jake in the surrey near the opposite sidewalk. To the consternation of his parents and the reception committee, Mitch's jaw sagged and his eyes bulged. He doffed his hat and trudged across the street like a man in a trance, much to the satisfaction of Sir Edward Roderick, watching from the rear seat of the surrey and Larry and Stretch, lounging in the entrance to a nearby saloon, nursing half-finished drinks and trading knowing grins.

"It *is* you, Kate!" Mitch could barely believe the evidence of his eyes. "Thunderation — I almost — didn't recognize you. I'd forgotten how — beautiful you are."

"How very kind of you to say so, Mitchell dear," she murmured.

"I — beg your pardon?" blinked

Mitch. He frowned uncertainly at the smug-grinning Jake. "Mister Jarvis, she doesn't — sound the same. And she's more beautiful than I'd have believed possible."

"Got weary of trickin' herself out in men's duds," shrugged Jake. "Decided it was high time she acted like a lady. Well, *I* sure ain't objectin'." It occurred to him to introduce the imperturbable gentleman in the rear seat. "By the way, this here's a friend of the family, Sir Ed Roderick. Genuine baronet — all the way from England."

"How do you do, Mister Firestone," nodded Roderick.

"My pleasure, sir," frowned Mitch. "Unless . . ."

"Unless . . . ?" Roderick smiled politely.

"Unless you're a suitor for Kate's hand," said Mitch, "in which case, Sir Edward, I would have to regard you as my rival."

"Oh, Mitch . . . !" began Kate.

"Be assured, Mister Firestone, I am not your rival," drawled Roderick. "As a matter of fact, I hope to return to England within a few months, and I shall be leaving for Omaha at the end of this week."

"Glad to hear that!" beamed Mitch. "So darned glad — I'd like to shake your hand."

"We have to be gettin' back to the spread now," Jake remarked, his tone elaborately casual. "Stop by and say howdy, Mitch. Any time . . . "

"Tonight?" begged Mitch.

"Gosh sakes, you only just arrived," frowned Jake. "Your folks ain't seen you since . . . "

"After supper?" asked Mitch, his eyes on the smiling Kate. "You'll be waiting?"

"Delighted to see you again," she murmured. "We could talk of old times."

"Kate, I'll be more interested in discussing the future," Mitch said fervently. "And I mean *our* future."

The day after Roderick's departure for Omaha, Little Jake sat a horse on the rise overlooking the Glory Hole, wistfully studying its surface rippled by the wind, while Larry and Stretch toiled nearby, repairing a section of the fence separating Double J from Hammerhead range. They were within earshot and eavesdropped shamelessly, when Dan Firestone rode up to the rise to talk with his runty neighbor.

"You've likely guessed by now, you schemin' old varmint," drawled the Hammerhead boss, offering a cigar.

"Guessed what?" challenged Jake. "I dunno what you're talkin' about."

"Like hell you don't. Your Kate is gonna be my daughter-in-law."

"That so?"

"And my Mitch is gonna be your son-in-law."

"Uh huh. Well now, Dan, that's okay by me. You raised a right fine son, you and Norrie. Gotta say I'll be proud to have him in the family."

"Sure. And that's how Norrie and

me feel about Kate. And I still say you planned it. All that tutorin'. All that purtyin' up. Kate's so all-fired beautiful, Mitch'd be hustlin' her to the chapel this very day, if Norrie hadn't insisted they wait till next week."

"Next week," opined Jake, "is as good a time as any."

Following his neighbor's wistful gaze, Firestone nodded understandingly.

"Still cravin' that hunk of water, huh?"

"I was thinkin'," said Jake, "now that me and you gonna be — uh — more like blood-kin than just neighbors. I mean anything I own is yours. All you gotta do is ask. So — the least you could do . . . "

"You sure are persistent," grinned Firestone. "Got plenty good water flowin' through your range, but still cravin' a half-share of this one water-hole, always callin' it the Glory Hole, as if it was somethin' special."

"To me, it'll *always* be special," declared Jake.

Firestone turned in his saddle and beckoned. The Texans quit their chore, swung into their saddles and rode up to join the ranchers.

"You boys savvy how to build a gate?" asked Firestone. They nodded casually. He gestured to the section of fence closest to the waterhole. "Right there'd be the best place. Make it good and wide. Rig some kind of latch, but don't worry about a lock." Digging a finger into Jake's ribs, he suggested, "We don't need no written agreement. I'm tellin' you, with these boys as witnesses, you're welcome to water Double J beef anytime you want. From hereon, you can call yourself half-owner of the Glory Hole."

"Dan," said Jake, his voice shaking, "you done made me — powerful happy. Anything I got — you just name it . . . "

"I could use a can of Wild Mash, if you can spare it," Firestone said on an afterthought. "For the weddin' celebration, you know?"

"I'll send you two cans," offered Jake.

"Hell, no!" countered Firestone. "Two cans of that stuff and my hired hands would be off duty for a whole week — instead of a couple days!" He raised a hand in farewell. "So-long, Jake."

"So-long, Dan," grinned Jake. "See you in church, huh?"

He watched his neighbor ride down from the rise and along the line-fence until he was out of sight, then turned and frowned at the Texans. Reading his mind, Larry nodded reassuringly and told him,

"Today, Jake."

"Yup," grunted Stretch. "This very day, old timer. We'll head back to the spread, fetch some lumber and tools and get to work on the gate. By tomorrow she'll be ready."

"Well, allright then," nodded Jake. "And, listen, you don't have to work out the whole month 'less you want to. I'll pay you off any time you want.

Only — uh — you'd be welcome to stay on for the weddin'."

"We'll likely do that," said Larry.

"But you'll have to act respectful — like genuine gentlemen!" Jake insisted. "Won't be no hoorawin', no brawlin' nor hell-raisin', when my Kate hitches up with Mitch Firestone!" He brandished a fist. "I'll deal harsh with any galoot tries to start anything! Even if he's double my size! I'm little, but I ain't puny. And . . . !"

"And you can lick any man in the house," finished Larry.

"How'd you know I was gonna say that?" challenged Jake.

"He's a hunch-player from way back," Stretch cheerfully explained. "C'mon, runt, let's head back and load a wagon. We get that lumber fast enough, we could have this gate half-finished before sundown."

The Lone Star Hellions nonchalantly saluted Little Jake and hustled their mounts down the slope, making for the ranch headquarters. Within the hour,

they would be hard at work, rigging
a gate that could be opened with ease
by the hired hands of Double J, and
Double J's fiery owner, now half-owner
of the Glory Hole.

THE END